ASSIGNMENT BANGKOK

Edward S. Aarons

Sam Durell once said his job was troubleshooting for a government agency so secret that even the government didn't know about it.

This time everybody seemed to know more about his job than he did.

This time he was practically dead before he started . . . a prisoner buried alive in a dark, suffocating cell in Bangkok.

No one was supposed to know he was even in the city. Yet only minutes after his arrival he was abducted.

Someone had known. Someone had been waiting for him. BUT WHO?

Assignment Bangkok

EDWARD S. AARONS

John Curley & Associates, Inc.
South Yarmouth, Ma.

Library of Congress Cataloging-in-Publication Data

Aarons, Edward S. (Edward Sidney), 1916–1975.
  Assignment Bangkok/Edward S. Aarons.
    p. cm.
  ISBN 1–55504–622–3 (lg. print). ISBN 1–55504–623–1 (pbk.: lg.
print)
  1. Large type books. I. Title.
[PS3501.A79A8928   1988]   88–4986
813′.54—dc19   CIP

Published in Large Print by arrangement with Donald MacCampbell, Inc. in the United States and territories; Canada; the U.K. and British Commonwealth.

Distributed in Great Britain, Ireland and the Commonwealth by CHIVERS BOOK SALES LIMITED, Bath BA1 3HB, England.

This One Is For
DONALD MacCAMPBELL

Printed in Great Britain

FW18751

ASSIGNMENT BANGKOK

1

He could neither stand nor sit nor lie down. The cage permitted him only to sit with his knees drawn up and his head bowed. There was no light. He strained his eyes to see, but he was wrapped in almost total darkness. He could see by his luminous watch dial that it was almost eight o'clock, and he estimated he had been here twenty-five hours.

The heat was incredible, and he was drenched in sweat. The air smelled foul, tinged with sewage from the nearby canals. He could hear only his own long, angry breaths gulped into his aching lungs. They had taken most of his senses away, except pain.

The concrete floor was wet, but he could not shift his weight to get out of the damp spot. He tried getting on his hands and knees, and banged his head on the low roof of the cell and scraped an elbow. He crouched, hunched like an animal in the blackness, swimming in his anger.

"Hey!" Durell called. His voice clanged and echoed in his ears. "Uncle Hu?"

1

He sounded strangled. There was no answer. He no longer expected any. Neither had he expected to fall into this trap. The fact that he was betrayed was no surprise. It was part of his business. He always walked with care and suspicion as his unhappy hand-maidens. You grew accustomed to watchfulness, to being alone, to hidden motives like the dark currents of an infested stream. *My own fault,* he thought. He should have checked out every room in the teak-and-thatch house on the *klong,* near the watergate, where he had come looking for Uncle Hu. He should have seen the light of fear in the old Thai bargeman's face.

They had come from behind, silently, when they hit him. Two of them he remembered vaguely. They must have been waiting. He shook his head, and waves of pain swallowed his thoughts. He let his head hang down and listened to the rasp of air in his throat.

In theory, no one knew that he had arrived in Bangkok from Saigon only yesterday afternoon, on a Thai Star flight. He had seen no familiar faces at the Don Muang airport. The taxi driver who took him along the fifteen-mile, four-lane boulevard into the city was garrulous and anonymous, as taxi drivers are the world over. He had ignored the

2

reservation at his hotel and chosen another, on impulse, finding a smaller room on the riverside mostly used by Japanese, Indian, and German businessmen.

He had made only one phone call before going to look for Uncle Hu.

Since then, he had been a prisoner.

They had known. Someone had seen him. They had been waiting for him.

He swore softly in the fetid, cramped darkness.

For a time, he simply sat with knees drawn up under his chin, not thinking, trying not to feel anything. He'd had no water or food since being tumbled down into this cell yesterday. At first, he had shouted and tried to force the hatch up with his shoulders, but it was solidly weighted down by something above the heavy teak floor. The old wood was like iron. Nobody answered him. Nobody seemed to know he was alive.

At first, he was afraid of suffocating. The place seemed solidly sealed and airtight. He had squirmed around in the tight confines of the area, exploring every inch with his fingertips. Along one wall there were a number of small holes as round as his thumb, but deeper than he could reach into with his index fingers. They had been bored or cast

3

into the concrete wall of the cell. The structure reminded him of a square, boxlike septic tank, but it had never been used for waste. Through the holes came a seepage of warm air from the *klong* in front of Uncle Hu's house. When he put his face to the grid of holes, he could feel the faint current of air that kept him alive, but he could see nothing through them, and no sound came through them, either. One corner of the cell was filled with crushed ceramic debris, as if large pieces of pottery had been smashed and left there. For a time he occupied himself by awkwardly trying to piece them together, to pass the hours of his imprisonment. He decided eventually that the pottery had been old *klong* jars, for water, and that his cage was an old cooling cellar for water storage, from a house that had once stood here in old Krongthep before Uncle Hu's more modern Thai house, with its gracefully curved thatched roof, had been built.

At first, he expected momentary inquisition or torture. But as the hours dragged by, he felt as if he had been buried alive and forgotten. Nothing happened at all. Time passed in his solitary confinement with no footsteps, no voices, no sounds of any kind from above.

He remembered the savage speed of the

4

attack, the quick rush of sweaty bodies, the face of Uncle Hu, frightened, and a scream from Hu's wife, Aparsa. He remembered blinding pain, angry grunts, and then the sensation of falling, the pain of scraping his body against the rough concrete, the slam of the hatch above him.

They had not even bothered to search him. He still had his gun and wallet, his watch, his passport that described him as one of the U.S. economic mission to the MDU in Bangkok, vaguely affiliated with the Embassy. General McFee, at K Section's headquarters in Washington, had arranged the cover for him before he flew to the Far East.

The boss of CIA's troubleshooting division had been grim and earnest.

"It is not a question of sentiment, Samuel. It is urgent. We want Mike Slocum out of the hills. He knows what's brewing there. The Chinese have come through Laos, from their military road out of Yunnan Province, and there's been a strong increase in bombing, arson, terrorism, murders. The Thai Third Army security people think it's heading for another split state, as in all of Indo-China."

"But we're getting out of there," Durell said.

5

"True, but just the same, we have commitments."

"Sir?"

McFee's gray eyes were harsh. "Yes, Samuel?"

"You say it's not a matter of sentiment, about Mike."

"Yes. But he's an old friend of yours. You sent him in, Cajun. It's up to you to get him out." McFee sighed and sat back, although his narrow, ramrod shoulders did not relax. Durell had never seen him relaxed. Leaning on the desk was McFee's lethal blackthorn walking stick, a portable arsenal devised by the gimmick boys in K Section's lab. McFee said, "Whatever the moral or ideological arguments, Samuel, we are in the business of collecting information and data vital to the security of this country. That is our job. That is what we do. No soul-searching, no questions. We need the facts, the statistics, the evidence of enemy intentions in order to make reasonable decisions for our defense. Because we do have enemies, Cajun, however much we wish for peace, enemies who are relentless in their drive to dominate the world with their system. We live in very difficult times. But I want you to get Mike Slocum out of there. Bring him out any way you can."

"Free hand, sir?"

McFee's lips twitched. "Be polite to Jimmy, in Bangkok, will you?" He was referring to K Section's Central there. "And wake up Kem, that Buddhist monk you put in as a sleeper. You'll need him. Jimmy will tell you why."

Durell, hunched and cramped in the stifling darkness, thought bitterly that he hadn't made the best of starts. On the other hand, someone had thought that his assignment was important enough to stop him immediately. He suspected there was more to the job than McFee had implied. And somewhere in Bangkok there was a traitor.

He had made only one phone call from his hotel, before going to Uncle Hu's to pick up the sleeper agent, Kem. The woman who had answered his call had a light, pleasantly accented Thai voice. "This is Miss Ku Thu Thiet," she said. "This is Mr. James' residence."

"Is Jimmy in?"

"You are – Cajun?"

He was promptly annoyed. "Right. And you?"

"I work for Mr. James." She sounded, young, amused, intelligent. "Please wait for just one moment."

7

He had waited almost five minutes.

Then: "Yo, Cajun. Glad you're here." Even in the few words, Durell could hear James D. James' cultivated accent. "Come right over, please."

"Have you had any word?"

"No, nothing from Mike."

"You mean Alpha Five."

"Ah, yes. You field people like the cloak and dagger game."

"Jimmy, you talk too much. I'm on my way, after one stop."

James, who was K Section's Central in Bangkok, and nominally Durell's superior in this area, spoke with a quickened interest. "No stops. I want to see you first. Briefing, and all that." There was a small click on the line. "Come over at once, old man. Relax a bit, eh?"

"While Mike might be dying?"

"Oh, come, come."

Again Durell heard the minute click. He said, "Your line is bugged, Jimmy."

"Not at all. It's Miss Ku. She tapes everything."

"And knows everything?"

"Perfectly all right, old man. She's a fine girl."

"I'm sure," Durell said.

He had hung up, angry and dissatisfied.

8

He sat with his chin on his knees, aware of his aching lungs in the dismal, warm air, feeling hunger and thirst and frustration. The hands of his wristwatch glowed in the dark. It was almost evening again. He drew in a deep breath and suddenly shouted: "Uncle Hu! Hu!"

He thought his head would come loose from the echoes in the tiny cell. He did not know if the cell was soundproof or not. He felt a sudden rage to escape, to do something. He squirmed around on his knees, got his shoulders under the hatch, and slapped upward, again and again, feeling his skin abrade, his coat tear, his spine jolt with the effort. He could not get enough leverage to loosen anything. The solid teak plank that plugged the entrance did not move a millimeter. He kept at it, panting and cursing. He sat back, slid down on his spine, and doubled his legs upward and tried kicking. It was a little better. Still not enough leverage, but it was easier on his shoes than on his shoulders. He drummed away, thrusting, sweating, grunting.

Nothing happened.

Then, in the middle of this, someone whispered, *"Nai* Durell?"

He did not believe it. He froze on his back

like a trapped fly in the odorous cell. He listened.

"Durell? You hear me?"

He twisted about. The voice was not imagined. It was a woman, gentle and frightened. He groped for the series of airholes in the wall and put his ear to them.

"Aparsa?"

"Yes. I am Hu's wife."

"Listen, please, I don't know what happened, but you have to get me out of here."

"Hush. You must hurry. They are eating now – the men who came into the house."

"Is Uncle Hu all right?"

"They beat him, all the time. He lives."

"And you?"

There was a pause. "I must go. You can get out. But you must dig. It will be very difficult. Dig, please."

For the first time, he heard footsteps cross the hatchway above him. Aparsa's voice ended. She was gone. He twisted about and sat down, hearing boots clump on the iron-like trapdoor. He thought he heard a man mutter in a Meo dialect.

After a moment, the footsteps went away. Silence was restored. This time, he welcomed it.

Dig, she had said.

10

Where?

He felt around on the muddy floor. It had been packed hard by generations of careful Thais who stored their water jars down here. His fingers clawed in exploration. He found one of the shards of broken *klong* jars in the corner and used its point to press down and scrape against the packed earth. Within three inches, the pottery shard broke against a hard floor. He felt it carefully, after scraping away more of the dirt. His hopes fell. It was only more concrete.

Dig, she had said.

It was hot, awkward work. There was no room to move, cramped as he was on his hands and knees. He knew now that the men who had imprisoned him were not far off. He could not afford any noise. He did not know how long he kept at it. The floor seemed solid. He could not penetrate the concrete. Then, gasping in the foul air, he felt the pottery piece break again as it caught on something. He got another and scraped away more carefully. After a time, he had the outline of a square, about eighteen inches in dimension, formed by a deep groove in the concrete. It was a second hatchway, this time beneath him, not above. He sat back on his haunches and rested, wiping the sweat from his face with his forearms.

11

Dig.

Suddenly, he felt as if time were essential, that he might be interrupted at the work before he could get out. He went back over the surface of the hatch. What he had thought was solid concrete was more hard-packed dirt, in the very center of the square. He dug the earth away carefully and slowly found the outline of an iron ring. He did not think he could go on much longer. When he tugged at the ring-bolt, nothing happened. The block under him did not stir or loosen.

He rested.

There were no more sounds from above. He put his face to the air holes and breathed in the clammy draft that came from the nearby canal. After a while, he went back to work, scraping away at the outline of the hatch. Twenty minutes later, it suddenly yielded to his tug. He fell back, hanging onto the block, fearful that it might fall and give him away by the noise. Cool, damp air gushed up at him. He gulped it in with gratitude.

He could see nothing below. There was only a ledge of floor left for him in the cell. He sat on it and dangled his feet in the hole. He could not touch bottom. If it were an old well, and he dropped into it for twenty or thirty feet, he was truly finished.

He took a deep breath and dropped through the hole.

He landed only a few feet down, not quite chest high, and he sank into wet mud. Quickly, he ducked down and found himself in a brick-lined tunnel, not more than four feet high, extending ahead into the darkness. He paused to listen. There was no alarm. Crouching, he moved forward, hands extended to find any obstructions. He did not think the tunnel would be very long; but it seemed to go on forever. Rats scuttled ahead of him, and he listened to their squeaks and splashings in the ankle-deep water. He thought the tunnel must be quite ancient, going back to troubled times in old Krongthep. The tunnel and the *klong* jar pit were probably all that remained of the original house where Uncle Hu's place now stood.

The brick walls were slimy and cool. Now and then they curved, first left, then right. It sloped sharply, all at once, and water dripped on his head from the arched ceiling. He wondered if he was going under a canal. He went on, his back beginning to ache from his awkward progress in this eternal darkness. Finally the tunnel sloped upward. He knew he had gone five or six hundred feet, at the least. It was difficult to think of

13

modern Bangkok above him, going about its normally hectic routine. It seemed unreal and unreachable.

He was near exhaustion when he finally saw a glimmer of light. It danced before him like a will-o'-the-wisp, and he was unable to define its distance. He came to a grating that barred his way. He heard the sounds of lapping water and distant motor traffic. The light came from a lantern on a moored sampan on the canal.

The grate was of wood, firmly fixed in place. He shook it with both hands. It did not yield. Despair roweled him. He was trapped in the tunnel. He sank to his knees and gathered his strength. Thirst rasped in his throat. He shook the grate again. Nothing happened. He backed up a little, then ran at a crouch at the barrier and slammed into it with all the strength left in him.

The heavy slats cracked, yielded, and he tumbled out into mud and tall reeds and fresh, warm evening air.

2

He stood on the banks of a wide *klong* under a hot, starry, evening sky. The water level in the canals, during this dry season, ran low. He sucked in deep, harsh breaths of the cooling air. To his left, at some distance, was the water gate to the Menam Chao Phraya, the Thai "Mother of Noble Waters." Most of the houses along the canal were dark, their thatched roofs gracefully outlined against the stars. He climbed up the embankment. The long yellow flowers of cassia trees drooped around him, and the red and yellow hibiscus blossoms looked thirsty.

He had come a long way from the house with its prison cell. Although the sky seemed clear, he heard a low rumble of thunder, and wondered if a mango shower was due, although it would be another month until the southwest monsoon arrived from over the Indian Ocean.

Durell searched his pockets with a hand that annoyed him, because it trembled slightly. His money was intact. Over the sprawling city that reflected a blend of

15

modern West and traditional Thai, he watched a sleek, fish-bellied jet liner departing from Don Muang airport. The plane screamed over the ornate *prangs* and *chedi* towers of the Buddhist *wats,* and at a distance, bright neon signs vied with Chinese lanterns in the streets.

He heard no alarm because of his escape. He waited another moment, then walked from the canal to the sounds of *samlaw* bells and the racket of Japanese motorcycles on a nearby street. It was still early in the evening. In the shadows of a tall *takhien* tree, he dusted and straightened his coat and trousers the best he could. The smell of white jasmine was everywhere.

No one seemed to notice him as he stepped into the racket of traffic on the wide boulevard. The lights bothered him, after his long confinement in the cell, and for a moment he felt disoriented. Among the pedestrians were older men and women in traditional cotton *panongs*. Girls were everywhere, most often with American servicemen and European sailors. Their tight miniskirts quivered, and the Chinese women looked aloof and wary in their slit *cheongsams*. Durell took in the traffic smells and caught a whiff of incense and a breath of spiced chili. He was hungry and thirsty, but there was no time for that. He changed his mind when he passed a food stall at the corner. He stopped there and ordered a bowl of curried rice and a bottle of Green Spot and drank eagerly and ordered another. The vendor was a young Thai girl who looked at him curiously, but said nothing about his muddied clothes and scratched and dirtied hands. Satisfied for the moment, he paid her in local *bahts* and walked on.

His left leg ached, and he limped as he favored it. Durell was a tall man, with thick black hair touched with gray at the temples. His face was sun-darkened, making his blue eyes look lighter than they were. He walked in a special isolation developed by his years with K Section. His hands were a gambler's hands, inherited from his grandfather Jonathan, who had been one of the last devotees of the Mississippi riverboats. He had been raised by the old gentleman in the Louisiana delta country of Bayou Peche Rouge, where he learned the arts of the hunter and the hunted. He felt he was being stalked now.

He turned left across the wide boulevard and then crossed Mutiwongse Road, with its Indian and Thai restaurants. He stopped to look into a window full of Japanese electronic gadgets and saw two shadows halt at the corner behind him. Not far off was the fashionable Rajprasong district, with its modern hotels and shops. His own hotel was not far from the old Oriental, with its riverside terrace, where Somerset Maugham once creamed up his yarns of another Asia. At the next corner, he crossed a bridge over the canal, which was crowded with darkened sampans and barges huddled under graceful areca palms. Gecko lizards croaked in the trees. A lute sounded briefly, like coins tossed into the oily waters. The plaintive notes were promptly drowned in a blare of transistor soul music, and he winced at the dissonant shrieking.

He could define the two men behind him now. Big and burly against the slight shadows of passing Thais, they maintained their distance behind him.

So his escape had not gone unnoticed. He had hoped for surprise on his return to Uncle Hu's house, but there was no help for it now, he decided.

Durell's education at Yale had overlaid his Cajun accent with an indefinable New England tone. He spoke a number of languages of Europe and Asia, was fairly fluent in Japanese, but he felt rusty in Thai and the Lao and Meo dialects of the Thai speech. His training at K Section's Maryland

"Farm" had so far carried him successfully along for years in his business, which took him through the jungles of the world and the dangers of the world's cities. He was a lonely man. He trusted no one. And he envied the simplicity of the people living on the sampans in the canal below.

Two weeks ago, he sent Mike Slocum into the restless northeast provinces of Thailand to scout a new threat to Thai independence. The Meos up there – barbarians to the cultivated Thai of the rich Bangkok delta area – were being influenced again by Chinese from Yunnan province, despite the alleged thaw in Peking. Mike Slocum had disappeared. In Washington, Durell had been sweating out his annual contract renewal, with a tricky leg as a souvenir from a job in Africa. He was not enamored by organizational work or by a desk loaded with synthesis and analysis reports. He preferred to work in the field; he found it safer to work alone. Mike Slocum's disappearance in the upland jungles of Thailand gave him the reason to shelve his desk work and fly to Bangkok. He would not admit to himself that he was breaking his own rules of ignoring loyalty or becoming personally involved.

Durell paused at the other side of the bridge over the *klong*. He was not far now from the house where he had been a prisoner. A hot breeze made the palm fronds clack overhead. He smelled salted fish, garlic, sweat, and cooking rice. Between the teak houses with their variegated pagoda-type roofs, there was a maze of footpaths and alleys. He heard the lute again.

The lane he chose twisted between the dark houses. There were few lights. The footsteps behind him scraped in the dirt, then came on more eagerly. He was pleased by this. His long hours in the cell had not made him friendly toward his captors. Maybe they were shocked by his immediate return to Uncle Hu's house. Since they had not bothered to search him, he still had his gun under his rumpled jacket. There was a narrow cul-de-sac to his left, a path that led back to the banks of the canal. He stepped into it and waited.

At KGB headquarters in Moscow, at No. 2 Dzherzhinsky Square, his dossier was marked with a red tab. He was also on the kill list in the files of the Peacock Branch of the Black House, in Peking. As a chief field agent for K Section, the troubleshooting branch of the Central Intelligence Agency, Durell's survival factor had long ago run out. He had seen many good men die, men who were competent in the business, merely because

20

of a moment's indiscretion, or an emotional diversion.

"Mr. Durell?"

His name was called in strangely accented notes. The two shadows now blocked the entrance to the lane. He could see Uncle Hu's house, from which he had just escaped. The two men looked bulky and professional.

He called back softly, coaxingly.

"Come on, come on."

"You wish to die, *Nai* Durell?"

"Who are you?"

"We put you in the cage. You wish some more? Worse?"

"Try it."

"You very stubborn man. We teach you fine lesson. You also foolish man. Why come back?"

"Come closer," Durell invited.

They were twenty feet away. The alley would permit only one to come at him at a time. Durell felt pressure move along his nerves. He stepped back, favoring the abused tendon in his left leg. There was a splash of water in the *klong* behind him. A sampan creaked by, poled by a thin woman in a lampshade hat.

"Come on," he called again.

The two shadows hesitated. He heard them muttering, too low to be understood.

Then they came silently, in a smooth, fast rush. Durell could not see any weapons in their hands. He did not draw his own gun. the biggest came first, arms up, his head drawn down on his thick shoulders. In his eagerness to reach Durell, he bumped the teak side of the house to the right of the narrow lane, and his rush was thrown slightly off-balance. His arm shot out, and Durell caught his wrist, pulled him forward on his own momentum, tripped him, kicked him in the back of the knee, and sent him sprawling to the rear. The second *kamoy* faltered, and Durell drove a fist into the wide face, felt teeth splinter under his knuckles. The man stumbled. Durell brought up his knee and chopped down at the base of the man's thick neck. He heard a rush of feet, labored breathing, and a grunt as the first man stumbled against his companion. Durell slid by. The way was clear for escape. But he did not want to escape. The first man reached for a knife, his face shadowed, eyes gleaming. Durell kicked at the knife, missed, felt arms encircle his knees. He went down. For a moment, there was a silent, breathless struggle. He used knees and elbows, broke free, saw the knife slash before his eyes in a wild swing. He rolled away toward the edge of the canal.

They came at him again, more warily. There was a low stone wall along the *klong* embankment, and from a corner of his eye he saw a wink of light aboard the nest of sampans under the bushes. A woman ran across the bridge, calling in a low voice laced with alarm. He took the next rush on his shoulder, flipped the man's weight over on his back, and sent him flying against the low stone wall. There was a thud, a low groan. The second man swung wildly and Durell ducked, came in hard, and drove him against the side of the wooden house. He slammed his forearm against the other's throat and squeezed hard. The Chinese gasped, his eyes bulged, and his hands clawed up to free his breathing. Durell kneed him, chopped at the side of his neck, and dropped him face down in the dust alongside the canal. The man curled up in a ball, hugging his groin.

The first *kamoy* had vanished, sliding over the wall into the *klong*.

"All right," Durell said. He drew a deep breath. His leg ached. He had torn the shoulder of his suit, but he felt eminently satisfied. His tensions were gone, eased by the conflict. The man he had dropped got slowly on all fours, retching in the dirt. Durell pulled him half erect by his thick hair. "What did you want?"

The Chinese shook his head, his face anguished. He was young, wearing a striped lavender shirt and denim slacks. His broad face was bloody. Durell hit him hard in the belly. The man fell back, hair in a curtain over his face.

"Where is Uncle Hu?" Durell asked quietly.

The man's mouth gaped open.

"Why were you waiting for me there?" Durell asked.

"No speak –"

"You'll speak," Durell promised. He hit the *kamoy* again. He remembered the concrete cell, the blow on the back of his head, the dreary hours in the narrow darkness. He put all his strength into the blow. The man's breath came out with a gush and he fell and rolled over, legs twitching, then drew up his knees and lay on his side, his mouth open. Blood trickled from his big teeth.

"Did you kill Uncle Hu?"

"No. Not finished."

"Why were you there?"

"Just ordered to go, to wait for you."

"*Who* ordered you?"

"To teach you bad lesson."

"Just to rough me up? Warn me out of Bangkok?"

24

"Yes, yes. But I just do orders."

"Who do you work for?"

"Muang Thrup Union."

"The labor organization?"

"Yes, yes."

"Run by Chuk?"

"Chuk, he boss."

"Chuk sent you to Hu's to wait for me?"

"I get orders. Not know from who."

"You're one of the goons? The tong people?"

"No tong. Legitimate union of oppressed laborers –"

Durell did not think the man was lying too much. He stepped back. The Muang Thrup was a Chinese outfit that ran the labor forces in the sprawling rice and teak mills along the river in Bangkok and the delta.

"All right," he said. "Get going."

"My friend – in the canal –"

"Tell Mr. Chuck I'm coming to see him."

The Chinese wiped his bloody mouth with the back of his hand and sat up, wriggling away from Durell. He rubbed his throat. "Yankee imperialist spy, you die, you stay Bangkok."

"I won't die alone," Durell promised.

Voices rang up and down the mirrored ribbon of the *klong*. Lights went on here and there. A royal police siren hooted, far away.

The Chinese got on all fours, staggered to his feet, then stumbled up the lane and vanished into the larger alley beyond. Durell walked to the stone embankment of the canal. The man in a coolie hat on one of the moored sampans at the water gate called to him in an agitated voice. Durell stood in the shadow of a leaning palm and looked over the wall. The water was black and oily, speckled with refuse. A thin piling and sturdy bamboo stakes stood up from the surface, and one of the stakes was topped by a large, black sagging object like a giant insect skewered on a massive pin.

It was the body of the first *kamoy* who had gone headlong over the wall. Durell watched it for a moment. The only movement was a faint swaying of the legs, hanging in the water up to the knees.

The hooting of the siren came nearer. He sighed and walked back to the alley. Police lights flashed on the bridge. A babble of excited voices filled the night.

He turned right and walked alongside the canal and came to the house of Uncle Hu, which he had entered almost twenty-four hours before.

3

The dark house stood a little apart from its
neighbors on the crowded embankment.
There was a tiny garden and a doll-like
replica of the home, mounted on a pole at
eye-level, known to Thais as the *sala phra
phum,* the abode of Chao Thi, who always
faced north in his duties as guardian spirit
of the house. It was a jewellike structure with
a stone platform on which were offerings of
tea and nuts and incense sticks to placate the
phi spirits. Durell halted in the shadows just
inside the low gate, under the straight trunk
and fan-shaped top of an areca palm. Two
klong jars stood on the porch under the
sweeping eaves. The windows were shuttered
and dark. A TV antenna marred the
exquisite, sweeping lines of the thatched
roof.

The front door, built of studded teak
planking, was partly open. Darkness yawned
inside. Durell moved silently and quickly,
a shadow among the shadows, and stepped
in.

He smelled cooking, spices, flowers, sweat,

and agony. He remembered the room in which he had been attacked, off to the right. The floor with the hatch into the cell was there. He stopped and listened, standing among dark Western and Thai furniture. The scent of jasmine touched him, but he sensed something amiss.

"Uncle Hu?" he whispered.

Something scuttled softly away from him. He heard a patter of tiny rat's claws, and let out a thin breath between his teeth. In the rafters overhead, he heard a thin rattle of dry reeds where little *geckos* croaked.

It was a simple house, but it showed a certain affluence among canalmen. There were empty bottles of Green Spot and Coca Cola and a bowl of *somnos*, green juicy fruits, on the polished wooden kitchen table. There was a refrigerator of dubious vintage that gasped and wheezed on Bangkok's erratic current. From the kitchen window, light came from the sampans and barges still moving on the canal.

The house was empty. He could feel it. But something was here; he was not sure what. He went into the bedroom.

The woman lay on the bed like a broken doll, her work-worn face suspended in a beam of apologetic light that came between the slats of the shuttered window. It was hot

28

in here. The air smelled. The woman on the bed did not move.

Her name had been Aparsa. She had been wearing a *pasabai*, a pink blouse of Thai silk, and above the collar her throat had been cut from ear to ear. The bed was soaked with dry, dark blood. Below the blouse she wore nothing. Her skirt of green flowered Chinegmai cotton lay on the floor at the foot of the bed. She had obviously been raped several times.

Durell straightened with a long, slow sigh. He no longer felt any remorse about the man impaled on the canal pole.

He remembered her laughing, smiling, giving him a deep *wai* when he first met her four years ago. She had been a woman dedicated to *sanook*, the sheer joy of living.

"*Sawadee,* Aparsa," he whispered, "goodbye."

He stepped outside. The incipient thunder of the mango storm had rolled away to the east. The air smelled hot and dry. Something fluttered briefly against the tiny, dark garden, and it had not been there before. He crossed the grass to the *sala phra phum.* A slip of paper had been weighted down on its offering platform, among the clay dolls and incense sticks. A small jug of rice whiskey

29

held it in place. Durell reached for the slip of paper and read the note in the dim light that came from the nearby houses. He heard a brief blare of Thai music from the nearest house on the canal, then the sound was turned down. A baby cried somewhere. The heat of the night held dry electricity in it.

The note was written in a shaky hand, in English.

"My friend. I rest on my boat. Safe. You know where. I cannot help. What happened is a gift of the 'sonkran'."

Sonkran was the Thai name for a madness that seized men during this hot, dry season, when thirst clawed at the land and it seemed as if it would never rain again.

Durell put the note in his pocket and walked back to the edge of the canal.

Uncle Hu's face was seamed and wrinkled and emotionless, and his narrow black eyes showed no tears, showed nothing at all behind their obsidian facade. He gave Durell a *wai*, his hands veined and callused by his life as a river man. His English was simple, but effective, spoken flatly.

"You have had difficult time, *Nai* Durell." He wore blue denim slacks and jacket and straw sandals. On his bony temples, two blue veins throbbed. His age could have been

30

forty or seventy. His wispy beard was white. "I apologize for what happen in my humble house."

Durell stared at him and accepted a cup of tea. The sampan rocked slightly as a boat passed by. The only light came from under the roof of the little cabin in the rear. There was a heap of pottery, piles of straw, and small boxes in the forward area, where Hu usually peddled his wares in the water market during the day.

"You have seen your wife?" Durell asked gently.

"Yes."

"You know what happened to her?"

"Yes. They made me stand and witness."

"Have you called the police?"

"Not yet. I know you, sir. I knew you would come back at once. So I waited here."

"You know it was Aparsa who helped me to escape?"

"Yes, I know that. I told her to speak to you, when she had a chance. I was not permitted. It is my fault."

"One of them is now dead," Durell said.

The old sampan man blinked, his only reaction. Then he said, "Thank you.

These men," said Durell, "work for a certain Mr. Chuk, a Chinese who heads the labor union, the Muang Thrup."

"They are all criminals."

"How did they know I was coming to see you?"

"They did not say. They came only a few minutes before you arrived, and they threatened us, Aparsa and me, and made us keep silent, and when you walked in, they attacked you and threw you into the *klong* jar cellar. Afterward, they did much drinking of Mekong whiskey, and made Aparsa cook for them. One went out and was gone for much time, maybe three-four hours. They ask who you are, what I know about you. I said only that you once befriended my nephew, young Kem, who has been in the Sangra, the Brotherhood, as you directed him four years ago."

"I've come to waken him," Durell said quietly.

"Yes. Kem said that one day you would need him."

Durell nodded. "I need him very much. I came to ask you where he can be found. There are so many *bhikkhus*, so many temples. A simple question, and two people are dead."

Uncle Hu poured more tea with his callused hands. His old eyes blinked briefly. He moved unerringly in the dark shadows

32

of the sampan. In the distance, a police siren hooted, going away.

"I do not know where Kem is. He meditates. He is a good Buddhist, a fine monk. He wishes to stay in the Sangra."

"He may stay, after he helps me."

Uncle Hu stirred. His wrinkled old face moved a little, but his black eyes did not turn away from Durell. "Sir, *Nai* Durell, we are all grateful, for the time when I was ill, and young Kem was hurt, and Tinh, his brother, was too young to work. Circumstances would have destroyed us, but you were generous and gave us much money, and we lived again." The old man halted. "I know that you mourn for Aparsa. You believe it is your fault. But you must not feel so. You are a man who is different from us. Different from most men, I think. Aparsa has gone to another life, a better earthly shell, we believe. You are a stranger, a *fahrang*, to me, but I trust you, and you must carry no guilt for Aparsa. I will attend to the rest of it. You must go on and find Kem."

"Where?" Durell asked.

"Young Tinh, my other nephew, knows where to find his holy brother. They were always close. Tinh is a boxer now. He is very good, they tell me." The old man closed his eyes briefly. "He fights tonight, at the

33

stadium. Mr. Chuk, who has many interests, also owns him. Mr. Chuk will be watching the fight, too. Go and ask Tinh. He will tell you where to find his brother."

Durell finished his tea. He took the cup and put it in a box beside the tiny charcoal stove. He thought of the woman lying dead in the darkened house, with her throat cut, and he wondered how long she had been Hu's wife. He could offer no condolence, no sympathy. It was one of the difficult aspects of his business, when laymen were involved and innocents were drawn into the dark web of violence in which he lived. Nothing could be done about it. He could give Hu nothing except silence and privacy. He stood up, and the sampan rocked a little under his weight.

"I will go to ask Tinh, then," he said.

"Do so," said the old man. "Let nothing be wasted."

Durell stepped from the sampan to the bank of the canal, walked in the shadows of the *takhien* trees and smelled the jasmine again. He paused before the miniature spirit-house in the garden and took some money from his wallet and stuffed it inside. Uncle Hu would find it. It might not placate the *phis* who had witnessed tragedy here, but it would help the old man. He would

34

have to arrange his expenses to account for it.

Turning away, he walked up the lane to find a taxi.

4

The taxi took him along the overpass in the Pratunam District, past the BOAC building, then on a run to the Chulalongkorn University and the Chao Phraya River. His hotel, the Ubol Duong, fronted the water, distant enough from the concrete and glass architecture of the more modern hostelries to satisfy Durell. The Ubol Duong catered to businessmen, not tourists, and gave him the privacy he needed. The lobby had high, ornate ceilings, cooled with large wooden rotating fans, and the bar had reasonably good bourbon, *Mekong,* whiskey, and a small Filipino combo that hacked out their versions of New Orleans jazz, soul, and an occasional dip into Tahitian-type lullabies. There was a tiny dance floor, and the management provided delicate Thai girls and some Chinese taxi dancers for private entertainment.

Durell ordered a bottle of bourbon and took it with him in the open-cage elevator that creaked upward above the potted palms in the lobby. No one among the turbaned Sikhs and West German engineers in the lobby spared him a second look. No *kamoys*, thugs, waited for him. And no police. He was relieved.

He showered in scalding water and mixed some of the bourbon with mineral water for a drink, then chose a fresh shirt and dark blue necktie from his battered travel bag. It was not yet ten o'clock in the evening. From the high windows came sluggish traffic noises – *samlaw* bells, the shuffling of pedestrians along the river front, where elegant white yachts were moored beside water taxis and rice barges. He cleaned his gun and dropped extra cartridges into his pocket, added a small, heavy sleeve knife to his right arm, and then stood on a chair and from the wooden fan in the ceiling, just above the bulky motor, he took down a tiny tape recorder and started it going.

He spoke quietly into it, recording his attempt to find the sleeper agent, Kem Pasah Borovit, who had been living as a *bhikkhu*, a Buddhist monk, for four years under K Section's orders. He noted his imprisonment, his references to Mr. Chuk and his bully boys, and then hid the tiny mechanism again above the fan motor.

The telephone rang.

No one, in theory, knew he had checked into this hotel. He ignored the rings and examined the two tall windows facing the river embankment, flipped back the cushions on two Bombay chairs, and opened the brown teak wardrobe. The phone kept up its clamor. He felt his way down the back of the high Chinese bed, his fingers moving swiftly. Almost at the floor, he found a small metal attachment and a length of wire. He pulled it lose, saw it was a tiny microphone bug, then tore it entirely free and dropped the transistor into his shirt pocket.

The telephone had gone silent.

He picked out a dark blue linen jacket, changed his wet shoes, and was ready to go out again when the phone rang once more. This time he lifted the receiver, but said nothing.

"Sam?" It was a woman's voice. "Sam, is it you?"

"Hello, Benjie."

"By Buddha's navel, what's the matter with you?"

"Nothing, Benjie. How did you know I was in town?"

37

"Everybody knows, Cajun. Listen, I must see you."

"I'm busy," he said bluntly.

"This is your business, Cajun." The voice was fairly deep for a woman, crisp and taut, without the usual overtones and inflections that a woman uses when talking to a man. "I must see you and discuss things with you."

"Is it about Mike?"

"Of course it's about Mike."

"I thought you were through with your brother."

"I owe him something. Loyalty, maybe. Pity. You name it. It disturbs me, and I've got to do something about him."

"That's why I'm here."

"Good, then. Come see me." It was an order.

"Where?"

"I'm going to the sawmill," Benjie Slocum said. "The foreman is drunk, and one of the sawyers got his arm sliced off, the idiot. Can you meet me there? You've been at the mill before, haven't you? Remember, a few years ago –"

"I remember. Have you heard from Mike?"

Benjie Slocum's crisp voice hesitated. "That's the whole thing. You sent him in. He simply hasn't come back."

38

"No word at all?"

"Nothing."

"Give me a couple of hours."

"All right, Sam. It will be good to see you. I've got your favorite bourbon."

"Mekong will do just fine."

She rang off. Durell held the phone for a moment, then cradled it thoughtfully. He stood for a full minute, thinking it out.

He had no difficulty recalling Benjamina Slocum. It was her inherited money that started her brother Mike here in Thailand, lifting him from a light-hearted, devil-may-care charter pilot in a mortgaged Piper Apache to a big businessman, with interests in rubber down in the Kra Isthmus, teak forests and lumbering up near Chiengmai, a tea plantation in the northern highlands by the Laotian border, and the Thai Star Air & Shipping Co. that had run Benjie's stake into millions. Whatever their prosperity, however, Mike remained the same. He did odd jobs for K Section, and two weeks ago, in Washington, Durell had yielded to Mike's plea for action. Big business bored him, he said. Durell suspected that his efficient, strict older sister also bored him. He had agreed to send Mike into the northeast in a Thai Star plane for the job.

According to General McFee, there were

fresh Chinese incursions from Laos. Among the thirty or more hill tribes, Meo, Karen, Lahu, Musso, and Ko people, each with their distinctive cultures and slash-and-burn agronomy, and with a penchant for growing opium above the five thousand-foot level, there was a growing defiance of Bangkok and a flood of arms that could mean another divided country in Indo-China. It was a mission to gather information, nothing more, according to strict White House directives, McFee had said. Durell still did not know what had gone wrong with it. With Mike's business connections up there, it should have been routine. But Mike hadn't come back.

Durell sighed, snapped off the lights, locked his hotel room door, and left.

5

"I am ordinarily not a betting man," said Mr. Chuk gently, "but I have wagered one thousand dollars, Hong Kong, on young Tinh, the boy in the red trunks. A protégé of mine, you see."

"Why?" Durell asked.

"Ah. He is a true fighter. In any conflict,

the aim is to win, eh? The world is more violent today than in the past. To enter a fight – or a war – without the heart to win is to invite and anticipate defeat."

"And Tinh?"

"He is vicious and single-minded. He wins." Chuk smiled. "You are sitting in a reserved seat, my dear sir."

"I know," said Durell.

"You seek me, personally?"

"You know it."

"Ah. Ah." Mr. Chuk settled himself comfortably in the stadium chair. He was a stout Chinese-Thai, with a high, round belly under his tight white suit. A number of quivering jowls framed his round face. He mopped several of his chins with a lavender silk handkerchief. The air-conditioning in the sports stadium had broken down, and the heat from the avid crowd and the lights from the TV cameras rapidly built up the temperature. Bright reflections of Pepsi-Cola, Yamaha, and Sanyo TV shone in Mr. Chuk's hexagonal glasses.

"You seem to be in good health, Mr. Durell."

"Shouldn't I be?"

"You are extraordinary. Very direct. You proceed like a charging lion straight to your

41

goal. Stubborn, too. Nothing turns you aside. And here you are, seeking me out."

"You know why," Durell said.

"I admit nothing."

"You admit you know my name."

"Ah, yes. But I am merely a business-man." Mr. Chuk smiled apologetically. "I am only a middleman in the teak and rice industries, concerned with the oppressed laborers, you see. I am not one of your *luangs*, a royal palace official. My life is quite open. Neither am I an agent of the imperialist Mao Tse-tung, a charge to which many Chinese in Thailand are liable. It is the tragedy of our times, sir, that the innocent suffer and evil prevails. My business is simply smoothing the wheels of industry and labor in the mills of Thonburi and Bangkok."

"And you run the tong called the Muang Thrup."

"Not a tong. A legitimate labor union."

"You hire torturers, murderers, and rapists."

"Come, come, sir. You can prove nothing."

"I can. I will."

Mr. Chuk pretended to be appalled. *"Nee arai?* What's this? I heard of your arrival. You did not look like a *fahrang*, a Westerner, assigned to the MDU – the Mobile

42

Development Units who aid our farmers. I am in the rice labor business. Did you know there are almost one thousand rice mills on the canals around Bangkok? No matter. You speak so quietly, Mr. Durell. Men like you never let the mind or body rest, eh? You see all things around you, and are always quick and decisive. You bore directly to the heart of the matter. But you are quiet. Ah, so quiet."

Durell shifted slightly so his gun in its underarm holster could be reached easily. He felt the pressure of Mr. Chuk's fat arm against his, and he knew that the Sino-Thai was shocked by his arrival here. Two young Chinese thugs sat on the other side of Mr. Chuk, their faces impassive. He wondered if they knew by now of the death of one of their comrades, impaled on the canal post. Certainly they were surprised by his escape, his prompt arrival here. Mr. Chuk was the jolly old King Cole of the teak and rice mill labor thugs, and no more, so far as his dossier was concerned.

A thunderclap shook the stadium as the two flyweight Thai boxers stood in the ring. The rhythm of thudding drums and a shrill Java pipe increased in tempo. The only similarity between Thai and Western boxing was in the leather gloves and trunks and the

43

squared ring. Durell studied the boy in the red trunks, Tinh Jumsai. This was Uncle Hu's other nephew, he thought; the only one who could locate his brother, the *bhikkhu*, among the tens of thousands of Buddhist monks in the country. Tinh wore a red charm cord around his upper arm and a sacred headband. As a cymbal clashed, the two boxers knelt and faced the four sides of the ring. Tinh looked tiny, but hard and taut as whipcord. His black eyes were emotionless as he prayed to the spirits of the boxing ring and swung his ropy little torso in time with the screeching music.

"*Nai* Durell?"

"Your boy looks good," Durell said.

"He will most certainly win," Mr. Chuk said blandly. "But you, sir, will only find defeat in your mission here."

"What mission is that?"

"We know you are not an agricultural expert."

"Your information service is full of Yunnan fables."

"Your arrival here, via Ton Son Nhut Airport in Saigon, did not go unnoticed. Our Don Muang Airport is very crowded. You were lucky, during your wait in Saigon, to escape the nail bomb that was thrown when you were in the Plum Café near the Thi

44

Nghe canal. Close to the Bien Hoa highway?" Mr. Chuk was amused. He liked to boast, Durell noted. "Yes, our information service is good. I am a loyal Kuomintang, sir, faithful to Chiang Kai-shek. One of my wives is a Malay girl from Kuala Lumpur. Lovely child. But of course, you are a victim of America's paranoia and you suspect all Chinese of being Maoist agents. I assure you, I am only a businessman, interested in profits." Mr. Chuk's many chins quivered as he smiled again. "Violence disturbs commerce, and who would wish to make Peking hysterical, what with their bombs and vast armies? You really should go home, Mr. Durell."

"What do you offer?" Durell asked.

"Anything. Name it."

"No bargaining?"

"Name your price. Your life alone, sir, must be of some value to you."

"Money?"

"One hundred thousand unmarked, small-denomination American bills," said Mr. Chuk promptly. "A guarantee of your safe departure. What happened yesterday was a mistake. I see it now. It was not my decision, I pray you to believe me. But it seemed necessary at the time. Now, can we do business?"

45

"You're too late," Durell said.

"You hold a grievance?"

"Let's just say that I must satisfy my curiosity as to why the murder of innocent people was thought necessary simply because I have arrived in Bangkok."

"Sir –"

The two fighters in the ring were going through the ritual of the Elephant Dance, the Four-Faced Buddha, and making hex signs at each other. The air was gray with smoke. Durell watched young Tinh slide his hands on the ropes to ward off malicious *phis*. He could not have known about the rape and death of Aparsa, his aunt.

"Sir," Mr. Chuk persisted. "I live in Sampeng, Mr. Durell. Please come to see me. It the Chinese district, and although many Westerners consider the area a hotbed of Communist conspiracy, you will be perfectly safe. We may come to a fine agreement – profitable to both of us."

Durell got up and returned to his own seat as the boxing match began. There were no Queensbery rules here. Kicking, kneeing to the groin, elbowing – all were in demand. The boxers were as agile as dancers, leaping high to aim deadly blows with their heels at chin or knee or belly. Tinh's naked feet swung like whips, slashing at his opponent's

46

head. The other youth aimed at Tinh's leg, missed and took a kick in the back of the neck that put him down on all fours. He was up at once, dancing back. The fans howled. The tempo of the music increased. The stadium was packed with Thais in Western clothes, some turbaned Indians, and a spray of American uniforms.

A chant began. *"Sok! Sok!"* The fans were calling for an elbow ram. The noise reached a crescendo. The TV cameras followed the boxers avidly. Tinh jumped high, aimed his right foot at his opponent's belly, danced back, came in again, and smashed his heel into the other's face. Blood gushed. Durell looked down at the back of Mr. Chuk's head, at ringside. The Chinese was smoking a long, thin cigar; he watched the boxers placidly. Tinh's adversary had staggered away, bleeding from a broken nose. His eyes were glazed.

Tinh was merciless. He danced high, jumped, and swung his left foot like a mace. His opponent's head was almost torn off by the blow. The screams of the fans and the weird thud of drum and Java pipe mingled with a clash of cymbals as Tinh's enemy went down. The referee pushed Tinh aside. The fight ended.

Mr. Chuk rose ponderously and moved

toward the ring. Durell stood up and went quickly through the crowd on the ramp, found the exit door and a corridor and iron stairs that led to the dressing rooms below the ring. There were other fighters here, with trainers, lackeys, hangers-on. It took a few moments to find the room assigned to young Tinh. There were touts, girls, fans, handlers in his way. He asked a few questions, got some shrugs, and finally a pock-marked Malay told him how to find Tinh's cubicle. It was beyond a long locker room, equally crowded. The place smelled of curry and sweat. Tinh's door was closed. Durell palmed the knob, stepped inside, and saw Tinh in a dim light, crouched over on a bench near a rubbing table.

"Tinh?"

The boxer moved slightly, his head down between his knees. His muscular little back was knotted, and beads of sweat stood out on the nape of his neck and down his spine.

No one else was in the dressing-room.

Durell put his hand on the boy's shoulder, but Tinh groaned and clutched his belly and rocked sidewise, not looking up.

"Tinh, were you hurt?"

The boxer looked up. His young, round face was a mask of agony. His eyes looked blind. He dug into his stomach with clawed fingers.

"Bad water –" he gasped.

"Where? When?"

"Xu – my trainer – gave me just now."

The boy rocked back and forth in his cramped position.

"Look at me," Durell said.

Tinh did not look up.

"Do you remember me, Tinh?" Durell asked.

Slowly, the anguished face turned to him. Through the glaze of pain in the black, slanted eyes came a whimper of comprehension. *"Nai* – Durell?"

"That's right. Your brother's friend."

"You helped Uncle Hu – and Kem."

"Yes, that's right. I helped Kem. When you were a small boy. Now I am back, and I must find him."

"Kem is sacred – belongs to Sangra."

"I know that. Which monastery is he in?"

The boy convulsed and doubled over in a renewed spasm of pain. He was dying. It was a waste of time to go for a doctor. Durell had to learn what he had come to find out.

"Do you ever see Kem?"

The boy gasped. His face dripped sweat. He straightened slowly.

"In Sampeng – in Kow Singh's tourist

49

shop. He goes there mornings with begging bowl –"

"Kow Singh's," Durell repeated.

"Yes. Please. Help me?"

"All right, Tinh."

It was too late to help. Great rivulets of sweat poured down Tinh's face and body. His eyes rolled. His tongue came out, and then he slid sidewise on the bench and Durell caught him before he hit the concrete floor.

Whatever it was, McFee in Washington hadn't told him all of it. Whatever it was, it had already caused two deaths, not counting the *kamoy* Durell had dropped into the canal.

There was a flurry of voices in the corridor outside the dressing room. Durell straightened and sighed and went to the door. No one tried to enter. The group of men moved on. When he couldn't hear them, he opened the door and stepped out. He looked back once at the dead boxer, and hoped that Tinh, like Aparsa, would have a better life in his next reincarnation. Then he headed for the ramp and the outside gates of the stadium.

6

He took a *samlaw* with a striped canopy and a rackety lawn-mower engine behind. The night was still hot. Advertisements flickered in rainbow colors, spelling out letters in English and French and the long, horizontal Thai script. The driver crossed Suriwong Road, returned to the Chao Phraya, then swung into Rama IV Road. He did not think he was being followed now.

"Drong bai," he told the driver. "Straight ahead."

At the next fork, back in the favored Rajprasong district, the traffic was lighter, and in the residential area the low houses were set back from the road, with pagoda roofs and lush plantings making cloudy darknesses on the lawns. The houses here had large verandas and were discreetly lighted. A maze of lanes led down to the canal-side.

"Charamaya Lane," Durell said. "Number Twelve."

The motorized rickshaw nosed into a narrow street bordering the canal. Each

51

house here was surrounded by a high wooden fence, so that only the low, sweeping Thai-style roofs were visible through the fan-shaped palms.

"You want me wait?" the driver asked.

"No." Durell counted out enough *bahts* for the fare, and paused in the dark lane until the *samlaw* puttered out of sight.

He sensed the cats the moment he opened the ornate gate. At the carved and gilded door, he heard the music, too. The heavy bass beat made the air shake. Oleanders, jasmine, and hibiscus dotted the lawn. Except for the Thai design, the house on the canal could have been in any Florida development. A sleek power boat was moored to the dock on the canal. An enclosure on the lawn was made up of small cages, where the sounds of the cats came from. Durell let his anger go into the large wooden knocker on the door. He heard a cat squall suddenly. He didn't like the shadows nearby. No place was safe, he thought.

"You're a bit late, Cajun."

"So I am," said Durell. "Ask me in?"

The heavy door swung open. On the post under the knocker was a polished brass plate that read in etched Spencerian script, *James Darwinton James*. Jimmy D. Jimmy wore a brocaded Nehru jacket and black slacks that

52

emphasized his pipestem legs. A girl flickered in and out of sight behind him, like a bird. Durell said, "Company?"

"My secretary and companion, Miss Ku Tu Thiet. Lovely child.

"How nice for you."

James D. James waved him in with an elegant hand. "Come in, Sam. It's hot out there, not fit for man or beast."

"I can't hear you," Durell said.

James closed the door after looking out across the lawn toward the cat cages, then swung about to lower the volume on the gleaming components of stereo equipment on his bookcase. The moaning and shrieking that substituted for lyrics in this latter-day popular hit faded to a distant groan of adolescent anguish. Neither the icy air-conditioning nor the incense that spiraled through the big, high-ceilinged room could erase the presence of the cats. Durell looked for Miss Ku, but she had vanished. But there were enough Siamese cats around.

Their blue eyes watched him from every cushion, every chair, with a hostility reserved for strangers. There were a dozen, Seal Points and Lilac Points, Chocolate and Blue Points, and two Albinos. A Red Colorpoint was perched on James' silk brocaded shoulder. The Red spit at him, and James made a soothing noise. The cat's humped back did not go down.

"Princess Mai Pen Rai," James said. "It's a common Thai phrase meaning, 'Don't bother.' I have a royal permit to breed these little people." He made more noises to the cats, who continued to regard Durell as a dangerous enemy. "It took something to get a palace license, I can tell you. Siamese cats are different, you know – they were bred for battle in medieval times. Quite vicious, then. Still quite muscular, as you see, and devoted to home and master. Quite unhappy when anything disturbs their routine."

"I haven't much time, sir," Durell said.

"These Lilac Points are quite unusual. Fine masks, neatly defined, connected to the ears with tracings. Liu Phan, over there, is a fine example. Excellent gloss and coat texture, a long head, a wonderful wedge from muzzle to ears. No whisker breaks, you see. A dainty fellow, really, for a stud male, but small oval feet, slanting eye aperture – a true Oriental."

"Sir –"

"Of course, old man. Go away now, children." The Red jumped, the Lilac Point hissed and scampered away. James D. James' hands waved, his fingers long and delicate, and the other cats moved silently out of the room. James' silver-gray hair was freshly pomaded. He was about fifty, with a lean angularity, and Durell did not doubt that James held memberships in the Polo Club, the Royal Turf Club, and the Royal Bangkok Sports Club. He probably also maintained a resort cottage on the beach at Hua Hin on the Gulf of Siam, as close as possible to the Klaikanwon Palace there. As Bangkok Central for K Section, James was technically Durell's superior in the area.

"Drink?" he asked.

Durell nodded and James picked up a square bottle of Jim Beam. From a hexagonal Indian table inlaid with mother-of-pearl, he chose a *kanum,* a honeyed rice cake, and popped it into his mouth. As Durell waited, he deftly poured three fingers into a heavy-based goblet, lifted his brows, and handed the drink to Durell. Durell put it aside on the amoeba-shaped coffee table and hoped it would leave a ring.

"Are you in business with the cats?" he asked.

"In a way. The little chaps are amusing."

"And Miss Ku Tu Thiet?"

James said abruptly: "You've been in the tropics, Sam?"

"Yes. Africa, Pakuru."

"So I've heard. How is the leg?"

"Fine, sir."

"No, seriously, Sam."

"It was blown off."

"Ha ha." James was as graceful in his movements as his cats. His eyes were wide and guileless. "Why are you so late in getting here, Sam?" he asked quietly.

Durell told him. He spoke flatly, but his anger came like a rasp. "Everybody knows I'm here. Everybody seems to know why I'm here, too," he said. "And they're reacting too violently. Almost desperately. I don't consider myself that important. Everybody also knows there is a serious Communist insurgency up in Chiangrai and Nan provinces, and that K Section is interested in stopping it. But everybody also knows that the White House has issued strict directives for our disengagement. The guerrillas have been active up there since 1965, when Peking announced a 'people's war of revolution.' The Meo and Yao tribesmen are the ones involved, mostly. So why did someone push the panic button and start killing, when I arrived in Bangkok? It's all old stuff. The Thai Army up there is handling it well. Why did I have to send Mike Slocum in, anyway?"

"Good questions," James said gently.

"I'd like some answers."

"Of course. I'm sorry you had such a bad time of it since you got here."

Durell waited.

James popped another *kanum* into his mouth, then spoke. "You are under a double cover, Sam."

"Yes?"

"Your MDU – the agricultural mission – is the obvious outer peel of the onion. No one in the business is fooled by it, but we have to go through with the motions for the sake of the government here. Your mission to get Mike Slocum out of the northeast is the second layer. Everyone, as you say, knows K Section's major interest is the insurgency. Mike isn't far from the Thai Third Army's main forward command post at Chiangklang. It seemed to us that Mike could have been found and returned to us by the regular security forces up there. But he hasn't been, has he? We receive devious explanations of the difficulties. So you are sent in. All relatively clear and aboveboard, considering the wheels within wheels that run our business."

"So I have another job?"

"Correct."

"Did Mike know of it?"

"I briefed him just before he left – as I'm doing with you."

57

"Go ahead," Durell said. He still looked angry.

"Actually, old man, we're cooperating with the Bureau of Narcotics and Dangerous Drugs, under the direction of the House Select Committee on Crime. It has White House approval. Our own S Section identified almost two dozen opium refineries up in the Burma-Laos-Thailand frontier area, the Golden Triangle."

Durell sat down. "I've seen the reports. Some of this is now making sense."

James moved about like a long-legged insect, all silver and knobby legs and arms. "The Golden Triangle accounts for almost a thousand *tons* of opium every year, and production is going up. You know of the drug problem at home and in the armed forces – epidemic, my dear Sam, epidemic. We want it stopped. But it is protected by insurgent armies and by renegades, gangsters, crooked politicians and regular Army officers from all areas up there. Political borders, old man, mean nothing when gold is concerned. All this stuff is moving via Saigon and Hong Kong to our West Coast, poisoning the nation. I won't lecture to you about that."

"You sent Mike in to investigate it?"

"We know almost all we need to know

58

about it. There are two dozen refineries in operation up in the Triangle, making opium, morphine base, and No. 3 smoking heroin, which is being refined now to the pure white stuff.

"Most of the buyers are ethnic Chinese in the area. The product is smuggled to Bangkok here, Vientiane, and Luang Prabang. From here, by the way, it goes to Hong Kong on fishing trawlers and junks – at least one a day – carrying up to three tons to the Red Chinese island of Lema, a bit over a dozen miles from Hong Kong. From there it is transshipped into Hong Kong junks. From Laos and Chiengmai, the stuff moves in caravans of two or three hundred men and horses and boats down the Mekong. The price has been going up lately – a kilo of No. 4 heroin is now pegged at fourteen hundred dollars. We know definitely of refineries on the Mekong River at Ban Houie Sai, in Laos. And we also know that middle-level military and government officials in all three countries are deeply involved. Sam, we plan to dry up this source."

"And you had me send just one man in, to do it? Just Mike Slocum?" Durell asked flatly.

"A preliminary survey, old chap, nothing more. You suggest that the reaction to your arrival was more violent than professional. True. Very acute of you. The Red insurgents protect the criminal elements in northeast Burma, for example – in the Tachilek area, we've identified sixteen refineries that recently converted thirty tons of raw opium into refined morphine base and heroin. In Shan, Wa, and Kokang, the material is put together into these caravans by the insurgent leaders and transferred to middlemen in the rackets, and then it journeys to further refineries in the Thailand-Ban Houei Sai areas. We've pin-pointed northern Thai towns such as Chiang Rae, Chiang Mai, Lampang, and Tak as targets."

"How are the insurgents paid?" Durell asked.

"Weapons, mostly. Often stolen U.S. material. But some gold and silver rupees are popular, too."

"And now?"

James D. James ate another rice cake. His chewing was slow and methodical. His unwinking eyes studied Durell.

"Now," he said, "we cut off the head of the dragon."

"But there is a problem," Durell suggested.

"There always is. We don't know who is the head."

"Maybe it's a joint operation of a number of people."

"Not lately. It's too organized. Consider what happened to you on your arrival. Fast, prompt, accurate reaction. You are lucky to be alive, Cajun."

"But do you have any ideas as to the head of this dragon?" Durell asked.

James shrugged his shoulders. "That's for you to find out. It could be your Mr. Chuk – but we doubt it. He's in it, of course, but as a minor figure, we think. It could be colonel Lak, up at Third Army base. Or any number of *luangs*, royal government officials. It takes organization, a network of transportation, and a legitimate commercial cover."

"Mike?" Durell said.

James did not blink. "Possibly."

"But I was asked to send him in."

"With *you* to follow, old man."

"The Slocums – Mike and Benjie – have the transportation network, the teak and tea plantations, sawmills, airline and ships." Durell spoke quietly. "I don't like it."

"None of us do, Cajun. Mike is a lush, and an irresponsible troublemaker. A fine sister, but a greedy girl, concerned with her business empire, pretty much fed up with her erratic baby brother. She really runs the

61

Slocum enterprises, after all. Making a legitimate fortune." James looked envious for a moment, then waved a bland hand. "You look thoughtful."

"It could be you," Durell said.

"Ha ha."

"Or your little Miss Ku."

"Not funny, old man." James flicked back his sleeve and consulted his watch. "Mike is due on the air in twenty minutes. We'll see if he comes on."

"You son of a bitch," Durell said.

"Are you upset?"

"You could have told me he's been in contact."

"I'm telling you now. You can listen and talk, if you like – and if he chooses to transmit."

Durell sat down on a wooden chair with cerise cushions that matched the rug. He still sensed all the cats around him. Movement whispered behind a curtained doorway across the room, and he sensed Miss Ku Tu Thiet, too. In a moment she came in with a small silver tray of tea and more rice cakes. Her almond eyes slid over Durell and he felt as if he had been stroked from head to toe. She was a slim, lovely Thai, proud and immaculate, in a tight cheongsam cut from

62

the same silver brocade as James' coat. *His* and *Hers,* he thought wryly. The high collar made Miss Ku's face look like the Siamese cats'. The slit dress showed a round, firm thigh when she walked.

"My dear, pour Durell another drink. He needs it. The poor lad has had a difficult time."

"Of course, Jimmy." She made Durell a brief *wai,* hands together as if in prayer. Her smile was enigmatic when he shook his head, rejecting the drink, and she returned to James. "Jimmy, I have warmed up the transceiver."

"Fine, darling. That will be it."

Durell watched her walk out. He appreciated James' taste. He said bluntly, "Sir, the only contact I made when I arrived yesterday afternoon was with your phone. Miss Ku answered. At Uncle Hu's, they were waiting for me. Does your little friend listen in? She knows your radio, I see. So how did Chuk know who I was, where I was, and get set for my arrival?"

"Ku? Not to worry there, old man. Fine family. Lovely girl." James' voice was suddenly hard and sharp, like the unsheathed claws of his Siamese cats. "Come along and listen in on the transmission."

Durell stood up. Ahead of him, he heard the quick scampering of cats' feet and the thin slide of Miss Ku's sandals.

7

The house was long and rambling, filled with lacquerware, antique Sukhothai carvings, and silk tapestries. There was a delicate arrangement of jasmine in a Chinese bowl. Beyond a modern kitchen and a glimpse of a long, pale lemon bedroom draped in silk, there was a solid door, a short hallway, and a closet. Through the closet was another door and the radio room. The air-conditioning felt frigid in here.

The radio was a TK-89 model, a bank of equipment with three microphones and headsets that almost rivaled the electronic splendor of the stereo job in the living room. Miss Ku Tu Thiet was setting two wooden chairs in place when James ushered him in. A big clock on the wall read eleven-thirty.

"Please be seated, gentlemen," Miss Ku whispered.

"Thank you, darling," James said.

"Tea, Jimmy?"

"Please."

She went out. Durell watched her go and said, "Is she on the payroll?"

"Naturally. She's quite invaluable."

"I can imagine."

James snapped switches and picked up a microphone. "We'll see what we get. The last transmission was two days ago."

"You're sure it was from Mike?"

"Certain. But whether he's in the hands of the insurgents or the drug smugglers is the big question. He may be talking under duress. He may be forced to lead us into a trap. Or doing it willingly. As I said, both Slocums are suspect."

The radio crackled and hummed. Voices spoke into the earphones Durell clamped over his head. Cold air drew an icy scarf across the nape of his neck. Distant music came in, drowning out the dissonant ghost words. For a moment, he heard the louder voice of a woman exhorting listeners to greater effort for the freedom-loving revolutionaries of Indo-China. The voices faded. The music came in a low roar, rising and falling like the sea. James clicked his tongue and delicately twisted the dials, then leaned forward on his chair.

"... position twenty-four by seventy-three, sector Kappa..."

65

"That may be Mike," James said. "Recognize him?"

"No."

The sea of sound roared in Durell's ears, and a ghost voice whispered, "Alpha Five and Brooklyn Omega, the ball game is in the last half of the ni –"

Durell was still not sure, through the disruptions, that he was actually hearing Mike Slocum's voice.

"– is coming in. Have you heard from St. Michael? May Day is tomorrow. May Day is tomorrow . . ."

Durell thought he heard a sound of weeping. He looked at James D. James, who sat impassively at the transceiver. Miss Ku was a delicate shadow behind him.

". . . is Brooklyn Omega. For God's sake, help me! Are you receiving? I can't –"

James said curtly, "Talk to him."

Durell shook his head. He still was not certain.

The surf sounds and other voices whispering in distant tongues, a repeat of the woman's taped exhortation to kill, maim, and bomb, filled his ears. The radio was an open gate to madness. It was Mike Slocum's voice. It was not. Two weeks in there could change a man. Two weeks in the cages, two days of

66

joint-cracking torture, could make a man into something he was not.

The sea roared out. There was dim crackling. Then: "When is Red Fish coming? I need some Delta Four..."

Durell said to James, "It's Mike. I'm 'Red Fish.' From Bayou Peche Rouge, where I was raised. What does he need explosives for?"

James D. James shrugged. Durell picked up the microphone. He said calmly, "Hello, Brooklyn. I'm out of the net."

There was an abrupt silence. James cautiously adjusted the dials, leaning forward. The Lilac Point cat named Phan came into the room, leaped to the top of the radio, and sat above James, staring down with electric blue eyes.

"Red Fish? Is that really you?"

Mike's voice was suddenly loud and clear.

"Hello, Brooklyn," Durell said.

"Thank God. I was beginning to think – I didn't know what to think. Listen, I have to get out. Things are bad here. Sam, you said you'd get me out."

"Will do," Durell said.

"When, Sam? I've got what we need. The whole can of worms. But there's a project here – anyway, when, Sam?"

"Like tomorrow," Durell said.

67

"Is it all laid on?"

"I'm coming in after you," Durell said, and flicked off his microphone.

James lifted his head and stared. His pale eyes were angry. Miss Ku reached out for Phan, and held him in her arms, stroking the triangular, masked head. The Siamese kept staring at Durell.

James said, "He had more to tell us."

"It will keep until I get there," Durell said.

"You assume too much. Perhaps he had a gun at the back of his neck. He may be in a cage in an insurgent camp or with the Yunnan Chinese. Or he may be happily inviting you to your death. I've read your survival factors in your dossier back home, Sam. On the actuarial tables, you're dead."

"Then I haven't anything to lose, have I?" Durell knew that what James said was true. He watched the man take a cigarette from his pocket. Miss Ku was there immediately with a slim gold lighter. Phan shifted uneasily in her arms.

James bit his lip. "I've got it set up. The Air Force can fly you in a Phantom up to Chiengrai, and we've got some intelligence people who can get you into the hills. The Third Thai Army people will be available –"

68

"No, thanks," Durell said. "I'll go in my way."

"Nonsense, old man. Don't you trust anyone?"

"Sir, the answer is no," Durell said. "Not even you." He looked at Miss Ku Tu Thiet, who smiled and made him a *wai.* *"Sawadee,"* she whispered. "Goodbye."

8

Alone, he found a taxi and got off on a shopping street some distance from the Rajprasong area and walked past the store windows crowded with copies of Buddha in the Sukhothai style and primitive, up-country *garudas* and *kinnaris* carved in teak. Hanging from wires in the shop window was a miniature *naga,* the undulating sacred serpent of the Khmers. Passersby paid no attention to him.

He walked to a quiet Thai restaurant. The hostess, in a glittering gown, ushered him to a small niche piled high with bright cushions. He sat on the floor. He ordered *nam pla,* a spicy sauce on shrimp, and *haem,* a pork dish from the north. Along with it came bowls of rice and crisp vegetables. He ate hungrily, watching the door. The place was quiet, unlike the bustling eateries in the center of the city. The other patrons, all Thais, murmured gently to each other. Seated, he followed the Thai custom and was careful not to point his feet at anyone. He drank his hot, green tea carefully.

There was a small *pipet* band, mostly percussion, that played traditional melodies while small *chings,* cymbals, kept time. A costumed Thai girl played the *saw sam sai,* a triangular coconut fiddle with three silk strings. He ordered more tea. A small group of affluent Thais came in, wearing Western clothes. Durell ate and thought about James D. James.

No one handed out medals for the work in his business. In the dark struggle against subversion, terrorism, and growing violence, the men who fought were anonymous and unnoticed. Durell was not ashamed of his patriotism. He held no brief for those who leaped to cry calamity, who heaped self-criticism on the West, and who indulged Moscow and Peking. The world, half slave and half free, seemed always to totter farther toward self-destruction. Men like Mike Slocum did their jobs, not so much as mercenaries for pay, but because they felt it was a man's proper and honorable course of action.

He did not like to think that Mike Slocum might be a traitor.

After he ate, he took a pedicab across the Chao Phraya River to Thonburi, the industrial suburb of rice and teak mills, and got out a mile up Rama Sriva Road at a busy intersection in Sampeng, crowded with restaurants, cinemas, dance halls, and tourist shops. A poster advertised Thai dancers in traditional, steepled head-dresses, announcing the ballet that presented familiar episodes of the Ramakien, the Thai epic of the legendary King Rama and his brother, Lakshama.

Durell made certain that no one was behind him when he went on to keep his appointment with Benjie Slocum.

The teak mill was a sprawling compound of native thatching mixed with tin corrugated siding and roofs, a complex of big and small buildings interjoined in haphazard fashion along the *klong* that brought the huge logs down from their long journey that began in the teak forests of Chiengmai, in the north. Normally, the mill would be a roaring, racketing, screeching place, even at this hour. Now there was a peculiar silence, and only a few dim lights shone. The steel gate was

71

closed and padlocked. Great rafts of teak logs gleamed on the dark waters of the canal. No cat-footed lumbermen were out there, no floodlights shone.

Durell paused. A dirt road led down to the water's edge. Geckos chanted in the dark canopy of trees overhead. He walked to a smaller gate, where a jeep was parked. The gate was not locked. He stepped through and walked toward the low, slant-roofed building ahead, where a single light gleamed over the wooden doorway. He did not like to step into that pool of light. There was another door for forklifts on a ramp from the canal, and he went that way, following a path through brittle weeds and tall bamboo that grew alongside the oily, slack water of the *klong*. Inside, he smelled the pungent aromas of teak sawdust, sweat, stale curry. But there were no sawyers here.

A light moved, gleaming in the darkness ahead.

"Benjie?" he called softly.

"Is that you, Sam?"

"Right."

"Thank goodness. Come on up." The flashlight waved, showed him a short flight of wooden stairs, and he climbed to a small balcony and saw her tall form in the shadows. He followed her down a narrow corridor to

72

an open office door, and glimpsed beyond it wide windows that overlooked the sawmill.

Benjamina Slocum hadn't changed since his last visit. She had never been very feminine, preferring work clothes and slacks to lipsticks and creams. Her manner was informal and direct, her handshake firm. He noted calluses on the palm of her hand. She wore stained, shapeless denim slacks and a man's lavender shirt with thin yellow stripes, the sleeves rolled up to her elbows. Her angular shoulders were wide; he could see no contours of her body through the oversize shirt and slacks. Her long, yellow-streaked hair was tied up in a knot atop her fine head, and wild wisps of it went everywhere. Her large gray eyes regarded him evenly from under perfectly arched natural brows that even her efforts could not destroy.

"How is your leg, Sam?"

"Better. Everybody knows about it, it seems."

"Well, Bangkok is the end, as far as rumor mills go."

"Speaking of mills, where's all your help?"

She spread her strong hands. "Walked off the job right after I phoned you. The whole damned night shift, and I've got two more rafts of logs waiting up-river for the saws."

"Do you run this place alone?"

"Usually, whether Mike's in town or not." A shadow moved in her fine eyes. "Sit down, Sam. Want a drink?"

"No, thanks. It seems lonely, here."

She shrugged. "I do Mike's work, most of the time. He spends his nights at the Playboy, the Red Arrow, the French Club. He was never meant to run an industrial empire, if you can call it that. But I've got the rubber, the rice, the logging camps – and the Thai Star Airline still staggers along."

She led him into a rough, businesslike office lit by tin-shaded lamps on two wooden desks. There were battered green files, two chairs, cotton shades over the big windows that looked over the sawmill compound. Durell pulled the shades all the way down, and Benjie's mouth moved.

"Always the spook, Sam?"

"Who runs your labor force? You've had to cope with Chuk's so-called union, I suppose."

"'Cope' isn't the right word. Mike used to handle it, but when he did less and less, I took over or it would all have gone down the drain. It's like guerrilla warfare. Look at this place! Dead as a doornail, in two minutes. The saws were going fine, even after the accident I told you about, and then all of a sudden – nothing."

74

"It happened after you phoned me?"

"Yes. They just walked out, silent as ghosts. I couldn't even learn what their complaint was. How do you know about Chuk, that fat, wily son of a bitch?"

"We've met. You look tired, Benjie."

"I haven't really slept since Mike took off on his spook trip for you. We have a tea plantation near Xo Dong – bought it from a disgusted Frenchman for a song. It made a profit for a while, but now the Chinese have come across Laos from Yunnan and the rebels are busting up everything. It's been two weeks, Sam. I'm fond of Mike, even if he isn't much help."

"I know. I've come to get him out." Durell watched the tall girl brace a foot against the edge of her desk. Her wide mouth drooped, and she looked suddenly disinterested. She lit a cigarette and offered him one, but he shook his head. "The problem is wheels within wheels, Benjie. Mike is suspect."

She sat up abruptly. "Of what?"

"And I have to go in alone. No transport. But you've got the planes. You know the way to Xo Dong, on the border. I'm going to do this on my own, Benjie."

"What is Mike suspected of?" she repeated.

75

"I can't say."

"Do you believe it?"

"I'll wait and see."

She was angry. "Oh, you're a –" She paused. "Look, you don't owe Mike anything. He *wanted* to go in. He's still living in his crop-dusting, charter-flight days. He's never grown up, Sam. Is it bad?"

"Pretty bad."

"Sam, I've made some money that's safely deposited in New York, out of ten years' work in this country. Thailand has treated us good. But Mike doesn't want any of it." Her smile was strained, slow, and wry. "He's not a desk man, Sam, any more than you are. I don't even try to pretend to understand either of you. Mike lives for kicks, for the spook jobs you've given him. He went off howling like a banshee with joy, on an up-trip. Mike really wouldn't do anything bad, Sam."

"I don't know," Durell said.

"He's given me nothing but heartaches, since we were kids." Benjie Slocum couldn't have been much more than twenty-nine. "But I've protected him so far, I guess I'm in the habit of doing so forever. I'm sorry, Sam. Whatever it is, it wouldn't be for money. How bad is it, truly?"

"I may have to kill him for it," Durell said.

76

Her gray eyes lost some of their clarity. She stood up, almost as tall as he. It was hot in the office, and there were dark patches of sweat under her arms. Her gesture was hard as she thrust her hands into her denim slacks. Pacing for a moment, she did not look at him. He could see why she put Mike, off, even as a sister. Mike went for dainty Thai types, elegant Chinese girls, or the occasional immaculate, well-bred, blond American girls who showed up in Bangkok as tourists.

Benjie said thoughtfully, "Mike has paid less and less attention to what we were trying to build together –"

"To what *you* were trying to build," Durell said.

"Jesus, you can hurt. But you may be right."

He waited.

He could hear the tree lizards along the canal, the dull, flat bumps of floating teak logs, and the dim clink of the chains that held the logs together. Wooden beams croaked in the heat of the night. He moved the window shade slightly. The sawmill yard was dark and empty. Farther up the canal were the drying yards, where stacks of rough-hewn timber made black rectangular shapes in the night.

"Sam, listen to me," Benjie said abruptly.

77

"I want to go with you. You couldn't make it without me. For some reason, Mike got static from the local military when he went in. But I've got an old Piper Apache up at our forest camp near Chinegmai. It's got extra tanks, enough fuel capacity to get to Xo Dong. We can get to the teak camp on our Thai Star logging flight, which is routine, not thoroughly checked."

"I'm not so sure I ought to take you in, Benjie."

"I don't care what Mike's done, I'm not going to stay here and let you kill him."

"He may not have done anything."

"Then I can help you get him out of there, can't I?"

"Yes, Benjie."

He heard the sliding movement of feet outside the office door.

9

Durell held his hand out, palm down, to keep Benjie from moving. Her face was blank. He slid his gun free and took two silent steps toward the door. There was nothing more to hear. Turning, he saw that Benjie had taken an old Colt .45 revolver from her battered desk. There was a photo of Mike Slocum on the green steel files next to the closed door. Straw hair awry, a grin on his freckled face, he looked amused and careless. Durell looked at Benjie; then he yanked open the door.

There was a squawk of alarm from the three men out there on the crowded stair platform above the loading dock. He glimpsed brown faces, heavy iron peaveys in their hands for controlling the logs in the canal. Two of them wore reddish sweatbands around their heads, from which their black hair stood up in thick shocks. The third man was a squat, muscular Chinese in a white Western suit; he wore horn-rimmed glasses.

Durell came out of the doorway fast, asking no questions. The nearest man with the iron peavey tried to raise it for a thrust into his belly with the barb. Durell kicked him low down and drove him back against the railing, which cracked apart, and the man fell through to the concrete floor below. The second armed man jabbed ineffectually with his peavey and screamed in a high, ululating voice, meaning to paralyze him. Durell smashed his gun across the other's face. Blood spurted, a broken tooth flipped out.

Behind Durell, a gun roared. It was Benjie. She held it as if she meant business.

"Wait! Wait!" said the Chinese wearing glasses.

The man who had fallen from the landing was a dim lump of sprawled limbs on the concrete. The second man had dropped his peavey and was on his hands and knees, shaking his head. The Chinese said, "You ask no questions, you attack first – like the sneak imperialist exploiter of the people that you are!" He had backed a few steps down the stairs and held his hands out to show he was unarmed. He paid no attention to the two injured laborers. "Please, you must be reasonable!"

"Who sent you?" Durell asked. "Was it Mr. Chuk?"

"Ah, sir, Mr. Chuk is trying to help the oppressed working classes here, and he –"

"What do you want?"

"We came only to discuss with Miss Slocum the terms on which the men in the sawmill will go back to work. A hundred percent wage increase, fringe benefits for hospitalization, a pension to the wives of injured men – like Tan Yui Phan, who lost an arm tonight – and paid vacations, permission to allow the men to listen to political lectures on company time –"

"To hell with you," Benjie said coldly. "Go back to Chuk and tell him I'll close the place down before I let myself be black-mailed by terrorists."

"You may not have to close it down, Miss Slocum. You have much dry timber here. The men smoke a great deal. A careless cigarette, a spark in the sawdust –"

Benjie's voice was flat and deep. "Get out! Get out, before I ventilate you."

"Of course, Miss Slocum. But the Board of Trade and Labor Relations will hear of your unwarranted attack on the poor workmen, your heartless treatment of the people..."

Benjie cursed like a man. In the dim light, she stood spread-legged, her big revolver against her thigh. She looked tough, competent, totally unfeminine. "You tell Chuk –"

"No," said the Chinese sharply. His glasses glinted as he lifted his head. "I shall tell *you*, Miss Slocum. There are notes held by the Aw San Fu Commercial and Mercantile Bank, where you – or your brother owe a matter of one hundred and seventy-two thousand dollars. It is Mr. Chuk who holds the controlling interest in that bank, and your notes –"

"*Sam!*" Benjie shouted.

Durell was a split-second late for the warning. He felt a blow across his back with an iron peavey. The man with the broken mouth had picked himself up and swung hard. Pain was an explosion all across his shoulder-blades. He lost his footing, stumbled, went down, slammed into the Chinese, grabbed at the rail, and fell the rest of the way down the wooden staircase. The man with the peavey screamed and jumped down after him. Durell rolled, got one leg up, and caught the flying attacker in the belly Pain burned through his left knee. He stepped back, the leg buckling momentarily; then it held him. The iron barb lay a few feet away. He caught it up, rammed it hard into his opponent's body, and heard the bellowing roar of Benjie's big gun. The stocky Chinese tumbled down the stairs in a tight ball. The man with the sweatband groaned and went down, holding his gut.

"Benjie?"

"I'm all right, Sam."

"Come down here. Lights out. Lock the office."

"Did you hurt your leg?"

"Just a bit. Hurry."

She was not fast enough. He did not know where the other men came from. He could not count them all. They ran up the ramp from the canal in a dark, overwhelming wave. Benjie's gun went off again, but he had no chance to help himself. Bodies came over him in a bruising, crushing torrent. Fists and clubs rained upon him, and he went down alongside the Chinese. He kicked at one face, and hopefully broke another's neck with a karate chop, but there were too many of them. There was a roaring in his ears, and he thought he heard Benjie yelp in sudden anguish, and then he was picked up and hurried away among a thick knot of panting men. He still tried to struggle, but his arms and legs were tightly pinioned. They swept him across the sawmill yard toward the dark sheds where the saws were silent. They had Benjie, too. He heard her cursing like a man among the dark mass of their opponents.

Light blinded him. He was thrown down on a steel table. There was sweat and blood in his eyes, and he could not see well. Something began to whine, whipping up a deafening scream of spinning steel. He twisted his head. One of his captors grinned and pointed. The huge circular saw blade in the shed was going, not more than a few inches from his stomach.

"Wait," he gasped.

He smelled teak sawdust and saw the loom of sawed logs around him, and steps going up into the darkness of high rafters overhead. One of the men laughed. There was a spate of Thai, the smells of sweat and garlic. The spinning saw was a huge steel blur before his eyes. He tasted blood in his mouth.

"Wait," he said again.

"Yes?"

The reply was quiet under the whine of the roaring blade. The Chinese in the Western suit bent over him on the saw table. The man's glasses were broken, and there was blood on his coat. He held his side, where Benjie's bullet had nicked him. Durell looked for the girl, but the men who held him would not let him turn his head.

"Tell us," said the Chinese. "Tell us everything."

"About what?"

"Why did you go to Hu Gan Tranh's house?"

"To hell with you," Durell said.

The Chinese raised his voice against the scream of the saw. The steel table vibrated. "You wish to die?"

"Let me see Mr. Chuk again."

"You had your opportunity to talk to Chuk. Now you talk to me. Why did you go to Hu's house? Why did you speak to Hu's nephew?"

"I'm a friend of the family," Durell said.

The Chinese said, "I have no time to waste." He nodded to one of the men standing out of Durell's sight. The speed of the saw suddenly increased. The hands that pinned Durell to the table tightened, began to shove him toward the blurred arc of shining steel. He felt the hot wind from the revolving blade against his face. Suddenly he knew there was no hope. There was an implacability in the Chinese face that backed away from him.

Above the scream of the saw he heard the hooting of a siren, shouts, a series of shots. Feet shuffled uneasily around the saw table. The faces retreated. Several of the men who held him loosened their grip. Their faces wavered. The Chinese shouted angrily, but one spoke back, chattering with alarm. There were more shots. Footsteps pounded in the compound yard. Durell suddenly bunched his muscles and heaved up and away from the spinning saw. He broke free on one side, twisted, slid partly off the table. The hands that held him grabbed for new grips and slid away. He fell to the floor, ducked under the table, choking in the sawdust. There were more shots, more yells. The gang of sawyers around him ran away. Durell rested for a moment on hands and knees. His mouth ached where he had been clobbered by someone's fist, but none of his teeth were loosened. He heard a shouted order, and the great saw blade slowly whined down to a moaning halt.

He heard Benjie say, "Oh, Sam..."

He stood up and looked into the muzzle of a gun pointed squarely between his eyes.

10

"You are under arrest, Mr. Durell."

"What for?"

"Let us say you have been disturbing the peace."

"I'm an innocent bystander."

"Not so innocent, we think. Come, we'll give you medical attention."

"Stop pointing that gun at me, Major."

"Of course. Sorry. You were inciting a riot?"

Durell said, "I do my best."

The Thai wore a military uniform with the pips of his rank. A number of Thai soldiers stood about in the sawmill yard. Someone had put on all the floodlights. There was no sign of the wounded Chinese or his men. Durell was not surprised.

"You didn't find the men who attacked Miss Slocum?"

"We understand there was a labor disturbance here. The men are on strike, we believe. But your presence is another matter. And you have been quite active in Bangkok tonight, Mr. Durell. We are advised that your presence in Thailand is that of an undesirable alien. I am sorry."

Durell walked out with the Thai officer through the wide doors near the concrete ramp to the *klong*. His ribs ached and the back of his shoulders felt as if he spent an intimate time with a medieval torture rack. Walking, he tested his left leg. It was all right, except for some new twinges.

"Where are we going?"

"You are under security arrest. Protective custody." The Thai's English was smooth and melodious. He was a small man with graying hair and a smooth, boyish face. He introduced himself as Major Luk Ban Long of the Thai Third Army Security Forces. His smile was apologetic. "I am truly sorry about the difficulties you have been having in our country, Mr. Durell."

"You're a long way from home. You're supposed to be chasing guerrillas out of the mountains, Major Luk."

87

"My work takes me everywhere. Come, please. I shall try to intercede for you."

"With whom?"

"General Uva Savag. Do you know him?"

"That bastard," Durell said.

"Then you have heard of him," Luk said calmly.

Durell said, "He wiped out three villages up in Nan province, last year. Charged the tribesmen with being insurgents, without trial, just lined them up, men, women, and children, and shot them."

"Do not mention that to him, Mr. Durell."

Durell saw Benjie walking amid a squad of other Thai soldiers. The girl looked angry, but she gave him a wry, lopsided grin as they met at the main gate to the sawmill.

"You're pretty good, Cajun. A real tiger."

"You're not bad yourself, Benjie."

"Are we under arrest?"

"For disturbing the peace."

The road outside the sawmill led away from the *klong*. The gravel crunched under their feet. The moon was rising over the palms that lined the canal. Across the water were low, thatched houses, each with its own landing. The air felt cooler. He favored his left leg again as he walked.

A small convoy of army trucks was parked

88

just around the first bend in the road. A heavy limousine stood at the head of the column. As Major Luk hastened to open the door, the light went on inside and Durell stared at the cruelest face he had ever seen.

"General Uva Savag," Major Luk murmured.

11

"I've had enough," Durell said.

It was an hour later.

"We have not yet begun, Mr. Durell," said Savag.

"I want the American Embassy, and the Ambassador."

"What you will get is a quiet, unmarked grave, if you do not cooperate. You did not confide in the man you call Uncle Hu. You did not talk much to the man we know as Mr. Chuk. You found the young boxer, Tinh, dying of poison. You destroyed government property in removing a microphone from your hotel room."

"Ah. It was you."

"And this is enough for us to hold you forever, under our military laws," Savag went on smoothly. "However, I believe you prefer to tell me your real mission in my country."

"It's to confirm your own job," Durell told him.

"*My* job?"

"The insurgents in your frontier district seem to have a free hand."

"My job is intelligence." General Uva Savag paused. "As is yours. But there is something special about you, I think. It troubles me. I do not like to be troubled, eh? So you will be frank and cooperative with me."

"I'll give you the same answer I gave Chuk," said Durell. "To hell with you."

General Savag did not look like the ordinary Thai. There was none of the pleasant geniality of the Thai people in him. Somewhere in his ancestry was northern blood, Chinese or Mongol, from ancient conquerors of Indo-China's tortured land. Perspiration shone on his round, brown face. Unlike most Thais, he sported a moustache. His uniform was extremely neat, the brass polished, and he had a swagger stick laid across the top of an empty, immaculate desk.

A fan whirred noisily in the little office. They were in an empty barracks on the outskirts of Sampeng, not far from a highway from which came the rumble and racket of diesel trucks. The soldiers under Savag's command were tightly disciplined, and they kept out of sight. A blue porcelain teapot steamed on the desk near Savag's elbow. He drank noisily, and his obsidian eyes never left Durell's face. He did not offer Durell any of the tea.

"Are you concerned about Miss Slocum?"

"Not particularly," Durell said.

"But she is an old friend, I understand."

"I don't think she's any man's friend."

"Ah. You do not like her? And her brother? A rascal, a whorechaser, improvident, living on his sister's hard and persistent labor."

"It's not my problem."

"Is not Mike Slocum your problem?"

"I've been looking for him," Durell admitted. "He does odd jobs for me. We're all trying to help your country – if Thailand *is* your country, General."

Something flickered briefly in Savag's black eyes. "I will overlook the remark. You have had a difficult time since your arrival here. You could use some medical attention."

"Who told you about it?" Durell asked. "Miss Ku Tu Thiet, in James' house?"

Tiny muscles bunched in Savag's jaw,

91

under his ears. His eyes were malevolent. "We are both in the same business. Yes, yes, Miss Ku works for me. A lovely child. It is her duty to report to my intelligence staff. We are riddled with traitors, saboteurs, terrorists, Mr. Durell, who work for the enemy. I will not tolerate it, I will use any means, any tool, to learn what I must know. You interfere with my work. I will not tolerate that, either. I speak plainly, you see. Miss Slocum, by the way, will be sent home under protective custody. But you will be kept here. I will not soil my hands further with a *fahrang* like you. I shall turn you over to Major Luk, who will question you further. In the morning, you will be escorted to the airport for a plane bound for the United States."

Durell felt relieved. He did not think he could tolerate any more abuse at the moment.

Major Luk was in another office in the deserted barracks building, and through his window the lights of Bangkok made a pale haze in the night sky, seen through a screen of wild banana trees that had grown up against the outer wall. Luk was very polite, very urbane. He apparently ate at odd hours. He had a paper plate of Thai bacon and a bowl of pineapple and coconut rings before

92

him, and he was putting lime juice on a slice of papaya when Durell was escorted in.

"Ah. My apologies. You wish a doctor now? You look rather – ah – desolate."

Benjie sat in one corner, her legs crossed. She had fixed her hair, pulling it back into her usual severe style. Her greenish eyes told Durell nothing.

Durell looked at the girl. "I thought they let you go."

"I refused to leave until I heard about you. Was Savag very bad?"

Major Luk said, "You must make allowances for my superior. He is a dedicated man. Perhaps he goes to extremes in his dedication, but he has been badly treated in the past, especially by you Westerners."

"He told me that Miss Ku, in Mr. James' employ, also works for you."

Major Luk nodded. "She is helpful, now and then. Are you surprised? It is all in the business, is it not?" He sprinkled more lime juice on his papaya. "Come, Mr. Durell, we are not uncivilized. I believe our ancestors had a highly developed culture when yours were still swinging from the trees, so to speak. We are very proud of our Thai heritage. To us, you are barbarians, relatively speaking. Americans are General Savag's particular dislike, I am afraid. You do not comprehend our ways and customs, nor do you try to."

"Let's not have any lectures," Durell said flatly. "Just let me out of here."

"You must forgive me. You know I have orders to put you on a plane tomorrow."

"I'm going up-country. Into your security area."

Major Luk smiled. "You are honest, at any rate. I have heard about you, Mr. Durell, and read your dossier. It is formidable. I truly believe you may accomplish what you have set out to do." The Thai soldier's eyes moved, smiling, from Durell to Benjie. "But you must leave Bangkok in the morning. If you do not, General Savag will be most annoyed. I would not recommend that you cause him any distress."

"The bastard," Benjie said. "His reputation stinks."

"There are rotten apples, as you would say, in every barrel. Am I correct?" He turned to Benjie. "You are free to go. I understand you wish to travel to Chiengmai?"

"Yes. On business."

Major Luk said gently. "Ah, Chiengmai. Once a beautiful city, the capital of a Laos kingdom, you know, for which the Burmese and Thai people fought. Your teak rafts start there, going down-river to Bangkok?"

"You know it," Benjie said.

Major Luk looked at Durell. "It was once an important junction, in ancient days, for caravans to Yunnan and the Shan states. Now, of course, it is our strategic base for the battle against insurgents... and others. The *moi* – the tribesmen – are most unsettled. General Savag is determined to halt their activities. He is very proud of our traditions. 'Muang Thai' means the Land of the Free, you know. Over two thousand years ago we migrated from the Yangtse, pushed south by the Chinese, and we established the kingdom of Nanchao, on the Yunnan plateau, about 70 A.D. Eventually, Nanchao was destroyed by Kublai Khan, the Mongol emperor of China, in 1253, and we trekked south again to fight against the Khmers and established the Kingdom of Sukhothai, which means the 'Dawn of Happiness.' The first king of the Thais is our national hero-figure, Phra Ruang. His third son was Rama Kamheng, a warrior, statesman, scholar, lover, devout Buddhist, and patron of the arts. He invented the Thai script, too. You know something of Sukhothai pottery, and the delicate bronze Buddhas from the area?"

"I'm wondering why you give us a

lecture," Durell said. "I was briefed on Thai history."

"Of course. My apologies. Miss Slocum, you may go."

"What about Sam?" she asked defiantly.

Durell said, "It seems to me you still have a few Mongols from Kublai Khan's day with you, Major."

Luk smiled. "You refer to General Savag?" Then a telephone on Luk's desk rang. He seemed to have been waiting for the call. He spoke briefly, then stood up. "Excuse me. It is urgent."

He went out. Durell and the girl waited for a moment. Then Durell said, "Let's go."

Benjie was surprised. "It's too easy. It's a trick."

"No trick. He wants us to get out."

"How can you tell?"

"He hates Savag's guts. He's sympathetic to us. He told me so, when he mentioned caravans out of Chiengmai. He knows what my job is. He wants me to get it done."

"You're building a lot on a few casual words."

"The Thais are like that. You ought to know."

The office door was not locked. The corridor was empty. Benjie followed him out. From an open doorway down the hall came

96

the sound of high-pitched Thai argument. General Savag's voice was a low growl over Major Luk's protests. Durell gave Benjie the signal to go the other way. At the head of some stairs going down there was a dim light, and below was an open door going outside. The sounds of highway traffic seemed louder.

"They must have my jeep here," Benjie whispered.

They went silently down the stairs. There was no alarm. The single unshaded lamp made a dangerous pool of illumination, and from behind them came the continued argument in Savag's office. Durell wondered where Savag's platoon was posted. Then he took Benjie's hand, and, together, they ran across the lighted hall and out the doorway.

Among the weeds and trash that littered the barracks area, they felt isolated, as if the place were deserted. Then Durell noted a cigarette glow near the sagging gate posts that led to a rutted road going toward the highway. Headlights flared from the traffic there, above a small rise clumped with vegetation. He pulled Benjie silently to the left, around a corner of the sagging doorway, and exhaled softly.

Two army trucks and Benjie's jeep were parked in the shadows under some leaning palm trees. She dug into the hip pocket of her baggy blue denims.

"I have a spare key," she whispered.

They ran for it. If any of the soldiers in the shadows of the wire gate saw them, they gave no sign. Benjie tumbled in behind the wheel, jabbed the key into the lock, and switched on the engine. The racket sounded enormous. Over its roar, Durell thought he heard a shout of alarm, but Benjie paid no attention. The jeep swung in a wild turn that kicked up a cloud of dark dust around them, and then she switched on the headlights. The guards at the gate were caught by surprise in the glare. Benjie tramped on the gas. One of the soldiers tried to raise his rifle, but he was sideswiped by the jeep and sent sprawling into the dust. Before any shots could be fired, they were through and heading for the open highway.

The barracks was only a few hundred yards along an access road to the four-lane thoroughfare. There was a lot of military traffic going east out of Bangkok. Benjie slammed on the brakes to avoid crashing into a troop-carrier. The column seemed endless. The jeep rocked on its springs, and Durell looked back. Some lights were going on in the rambling barracks. A single shot made a dim popping noise, through the racket of the traffic, but the bullet went wide.

Benjie grinned wanly. "Major Luk is not going to be very comfortable when Savag learns of this."

"I'm sure Luk has an explanation ready for the general."

There was a momentary gap in the convoy. Benjie stepped on the gas and the jeep bounced forward onto the concrete. She swung left, tires screeching, and headed for the city. Durell looked backward, but no one seemed to be following. If he had estimated Uva Savag correctly, however, the general would be turning the town upside down for him.

"Are you still willing to fly me to Chiengmai?"

Benjie looked serious. "On my deal. I go with you."

Durell considered it. The girl was competent enough. On the other hand, she was a sure tell-tale for General Savag to take him in again. "Can you get a plane to the airport?"

"There's a small strip at Lung Moc. I'll have a Thai Star plane there by dawn. But where will you stay tonight?"

"Better if you don't know. I'll be at Lung

Moc before ten in the morning," Durell decided.

Headlights flared behind them on the highway, but as they passed into the outskirts of Sampeng, heading for the Chao Phraya River, he saw no special pursuit. When Benjie spoke again, her voice had softened, but her grin was still tough and insolent.

"Sam, you make me feel like Goldilocks – only, I'm Mama Bear. Do you have plans to crawl into *my* bed tonight?"

He looked at her. She was the most un-feminine woman he had met in a long time. He spoke bluntly.

"Not likely," he said.

12

The young monk, Prajadhipok, was happy. Pra was nineteen, a *samanara*, a novitiate monk. The sun beat down fiercely on his shaven head as he trudged in the dust to Sampeng, behind Kem. Brother Kem was his idol. Everything about Kem was holy. His spirituality was a moral lesson to all at the little temple on the outskirts of Bangkok, where they lived. Pra carried his begging

100

bowl in both hands as he followed Kem around the corner to their usual stops at the tourist shops which, at this hour, were still relatively empty.

The day would be hot and dry. The monsoons and the blessed rains from heaven were still one month away, as Buddha willed. Pra was stout for a monk, although he ate sparingly, as all the brothers of the Sangha did. The Wat Kao Po was not a rich or elaborate temple, and it did not attract tourists. Its *prangs* did not pierce the hard sky, nor were their emerald Buddhas and yellow-tiled roofs meant to provide earthly beauty. True, there were the triple-headed elephants at the main entrance, and the tall central tower boasted a mosaic of shells dug from the delta mud, reaching for the triple trident of Siva. It was a back-country temple, but wherever Brother Kem lived, that place was sanctified. Now and then Pra worried about the joy in his life. All was a dream in the eye of Buddha that would blend into the next inevitable reincarnation that would lead, eventually, to oblivion in the Universal – if one were holy enough, like Kem.

Pra had risen from a lowly *dek wat*, a temple boy, where he received only board and lodging at the monastery. Now, as a *samanara*, he hoped to become a *bhikkhu*, a

101

monk who wore the orange-yellow robe. His hair and eyebrows were totally shaven. Life was austere. He had awakened this sunrise to the sounds of prayer and drums, and had washed, swept his cell, helped to broom the courtyard and filtered the drinking water, which was not to kill insects, but to purify it spiritually.

Trudging behind Brother Kem, he had marched out with the others, with his alms bowl. Already he had collected curry and fruit, which he had accepted with downcast eyes. Never did one give thanks to the donor. It would rob the giver of making merit. After the sun passed the noon hour, he would be allowed to drink only liquids. To eat, he had to push back his robe and bare one shoulder. He would spend the afternoon with Kem in the wat's pavilion where the resident monks maintained school rooms for the villagers. There was a Buddha image there of crystal, and another of jasper, and he would sit in the class with Kem under the symbols of the Teacher – The Bodhitree – the sacred serpent and the wheel of doctrine.

Pra often wondered that Brother Kem, who had seen much of the world and the ways of men, had chosen the little country temple in which to seek holiness and merit. Kem had even seen America, had gone to college there, with the help of certain Americans; but Brother Kem never spoke of that.

In busy Sampeng, where shopkeepers enjoyed the briefly cool hours before the sun really struck down, Kem moved ahead in his saffron robe with his shaven skull meekly bowed before the great glories of Buddha. It was a day like every other day. But the shops, the dust, the glare of light, the gay splash of blossoms, were all illusions. Trudging behind Kem, Pra saw him turn his gentle eyes toward him, smiling. They passed a clockmaker's shop and all the clocks in there began to chime the eighth hour of the day since midnight. Kem halted.

"Wait, Brother Pra," said Kem. "Mr. Kow Singh always has a few coins for us."

The Kow Singh Clock Shop was a dusty haven of quiet in a side alley off one of the busier roads in Sampeng. Brother Kem always went in alone. Pra never questioned this. He knew it had something to do with a vow that Kem had once taken, but what the vow was and why Brother Kem never failed to stop here on his alms-begging rounds was never explained, and Pra never presumed to ask for an explanation. Now, on this morning, like every other morning, Kem, his bald head agleam with sweat in the morning

103

sun, smiled again and walked into the shop without bidding Pra goodbye.

Pra sat down in the dust at the corner, his eyes humbly downcast, his bowl held out at the feet of the busy, worldly shoppers, whores, tourists and children who shuffled by.

There was nothing unusual about this day.

Durell had not slept much during the night. He had doubled back after leaving Benjie, and had chosen the sawmill as the safest place until dawn. The hotel was out. Neither did he think it wise to telephone to James D. James. Sooner or later he would have to warn James about the dainty Miss Ku being a police spy for Third Thai Army intelligence.

The sawmill was deserted when he returned to it. He had spent a tedious hour searching Benjie's files in the office that overlooked the compound, and it was past midnight when he finished with her desk and the green metal cabinets. He found nothing out of the ordinary. Maybe Mike and Benjie Slocum were innocent of involvement in the opium traffic he was supposed to track down.

The trade in narcotics in Southeast Asia was highly involved and complicated, convoluted like the coils of a giant serpent. Somehow, he had to find the dragon's head and cut it off. His body ached and complained when he finished his search. He did not feel particularly like a knight errant seeking a dragon. Sleep engulfed him at once when he stretched out on the floor in a corner facing the stairway. Nothing disturbed him. The night had passed quietly. The only sounds he heard was an occasional splash in the nearby *klong,* and the croaking and chuckling of geckos in the trees outside.

Now, at eight o'clock, Durell stood in the shadowed recess in the back of Kow Singh's Clock Shop, and watched Kem Pasah Borovit's shadow fall across the sunlit doorway. The clocks ticked and whirred all around him. There was danger here, if James had leaked the drop-contact point within Miss Ku's hearing. So far, there was no sign of it. And Kem, the monk, was exactly on time in making his daily rounds. Even with his shaven head and Buddhist robe, Durell recognized him.

He did not move in the ticking shadows when Kem stepped inside, among the dusty shelves and display cases. The monk's liquid eyes were serene. Mr. Kow Singh had conveniently scuttled into the back room behind the shop, where he lived.

For a moment, Kem was not aware of Durell's presence. The *bhikkhu* stood patiently by with his begging bowl. Then his glance touched Durell's tall shadow in the rear of the dusty shop. Nothing changed in the monk's eyes. A brief smile touched his mouth, and then he bowed his shaven head.

Durell said, "Hello, Flivver."

"Is it truly you, *nai* Durell?"

"Truly me, Flivver."

"It has been many years since I was called by that name," said the *bhikkhu*. "Do you really recognize me now?"

"There is a cloak of sanctity about you that wasn't there when you raised so much hell as a student at Williams, where you got your nickname, buying that antique Ford you used to tear around in."

"That was another life," said Kem quietly.

"But you made a promise then," Durell told him.

"I have been expecting you. I come here every day."

"I need your help," Durell said.

"I know that, or you would not be here. I have been waiting for many years. I am not the same man you knew as Flivver when I studied in your country. It was you who turned my life into the paths of holiness. Perhaps you did not intend for me to take the Sangha seriously. Perhaps you only meant to put me here for this day, when you need

106

my help. Today I make *tam boon.* I make much merit for my soul. I walk only in the ways of holiness."

"You were always a rogue," said Durell flatly. "You're still a rogue. I know you, Kem. Don't forget that."

Kem sighed. His face betrayed nothing; his black eyes were fathomless. Perhaps amusement flickered there in the memories recalled by Durell's words. Then Kem stepped forward and shook hands firmly, instead of giving him the usual *wai* greeting. Durell was relieved when Kem said, "What can I do to repay you for setting my feet on the path to Infinity? How can I show my gratitude for the blessings you have showered on me and my family?"

"Flivver, there's evil in the world, in yours and mine. Your family has been grievously hurt by people I must find and destroy. Your Uncle Hu, your young brother Tinh, your Aunt Aparsa – Aparsa and Tinh are dead."

The monk stood unmoving, not a fold of his yellow robe astir. His huge black eyes under his shaven brows regarded Durell for a long, unwinking moment, without any other physical reaction. Then he said quietly, "Blessed be their souls, for they truly sought goodness in their humble lives. It is the way of the Universe, the way of the Infinite Path toward the ultimate end of all our spirits. Was it because of your arrival in Bangkok?"

"Yes," Durell said bluntly. "They were killed because of what I must do."

"I will not seek vengeance," said Kem.

"I don't ask you for vengeance. I simply need your help. Do you still intend to keep your promise to us?"

"I am what you made me, Sam. Are you surprised that I accept the blessings of Buddha and am diligent at my worldly tasks? Even the worst rascal can reform, even the most vicious criminal may repent." The monk suddenly grinned. "When you call me Flivver, you make me wicked again. Those were good days. What can I do for you?"

"I have to go north, beyond Chiengmai."

"I understand. The Communist insurgents are there."

"Not insurgents. Opium."

"Ah," said Kem. "Very wicked."

"I need you with me to smooth the way, to talk to the local tribesmen in their own dialects, to exercise the weight of your presence as a *bhikkhu.*"

"There are thousands of *bhikkhus* in Thailand. I am only one of many. But I have been in the northern provinces, as I am sure you know. I am sure you have been watching me. Do you think you will be safer in my

108

company? I am a rogue, as you say. I pray to God to ease my soul of its remembered wickedness. Why should you trust me? Some monasteries raise their own poppy up there. One even manufactures heroin and sells it to the insurgents who manage to transport it down the Mekong into Laos and Vietnam, for your servicemen. Yes, it is a wicked world." The monk smiled gently at Durell, his bald eyebrows and skull making his face inscrutable. "How can you trust me, Sam?"

"Will you come with me, Flivver?"

"I will pay my debt. On the way, we will talk of the good old days, eh? Come."

They stepped out of the clock shop. The narrow streets of Sampeng were more crowded and noisier than before. The sun struck at the traffic and people like hammer strokes. Durell followed closely as the *bhikkhu* strode purposefully to the first corner. The passersby were neutral, uninterested. At the intersection, the monk paused. A faintly puzzled look crossed his black, slanted eyes as he glanced about.

"Where is Para?"

"Who?"

"My *samanara*. A boy who thinks I am even holier than the abbot. He has always waited here for me, every morning, like a faithful little dog."

109

Durell looked at the corner. Two old men were playing mah jongg on a wooden balcony over an awninged porcelain shop. Motorcycles and pedicabs roared and puttered by. He saw nothing unusual. Then a closed black sedan went by, slowing for a bullock cart that creaked across the way. Durell glimpsed the face of General Savag in a back window.

"Never mind Pra," he said quietly. "Let's go."

"But –"

"You won't see Pra again," Durell said.

13

They left the city by way of the intricate maze of canals and waterways that led into the parched countryside. An old sampan water-taxi man agreed to take them, greeting the monk respectfully. His eyes were dubious as he regarded Durell's tall, Western figure, but Kem assured him the *fahrang* was on his way to make his respects to the village *wat* and perhaps give a large donation. They followed a route that few tourists took.

On the way, Kem sat with his straight back toward Durell, his bald head gleaming

110

in the sun. Away from the Chao Phraya, the canals twisted tortuously this way and that through teeming tenements, water markets, masses of barges, and occasional rice boats. Women washed their laundry on the banks, and children ran and played in the thin shade of the trees or in the shadows under the stilted houses that clung to the water's edge. They passed riverboats piled high with brown, unhulled rice, tiny Thai houses with roofs twisted and sloped into linear dragons known as *"cho fa"* – a bunch of sky. There were icecream vendors, women with flat baskets hanging from carved teak poles, lotus blossoms, filmy black fishnets, small boys diving in the muddy water. *Samlaws* rattled over the bridges above them, old men sat and spat in the water, old women watched and chewed betel nut, laundry hung from tall poles, and peddler sampans tried to sell baubles and pots and a young girl watched them gravely while eating a green *somno* with the juice running down her chin.

The sampan had a small three-horse outboard that puttered slowly and diligently, and the old man who guided them seemed to sleep most of the time as they maneuvered from one canal to the other, going north. Now and then they passed a minor *wat*, some with elaborate central towers adorned with full-breasted caryatids, teeming with holy monkeys and carved with grotesque giants. The sampan man occasionally rang a small brass bell to warn another boat of their progress. Young girls chattered in the shadows under the innumerable bridges. One shouted something to Durell and laughed and threw him an orange, which he caught and nodded grave thanks for. The girls giggled and fled away as they passed.

Durell ate the orange, after offering it to Kem and the sampan man. It tasted bitter and strange.

Pasted to the reed door of the little forward cabin of the sampan was a clipping from the New China News Agency. It showed Peking's Hsin Chiao Hotel and a huge portrait of Mao. The newspaper was stained and yellowed with age. A packet of rice, presumably the sampan man's dinner, was wrapped in the Japanese left-wing news-paper, *Asahi Shimbun*. Durell felt the old man's eyes upon him and turned to meet his gaze.

"You American?"

"Yes," Durell said. "You Communist?"

"Yes."

The heat was oppressive, and the water level in the canals had dropped far below normal, before the coming monsoon. The sky was the color of brass.

The sampan man said, "The *bhikkhu* is a good man. Why do you go with him? He is a saint."

"And I am not?"

"You are capitalist imperialist." The old man's eyes glittered briefly. "But the *bhikkhu* understands nothing of that."

On the banks of the canal, they passed a small chapel where barefooted women came and went, offering flowers before the saffron-robed monks who sat crosslegged facing the wall. Kem asked the sampan-man to stop.

"I must leave a message for my abbot," he said. "And make an inquiry about Pra. What do you think happened to him?"

"Nothing good," said Durell. "And now you're on the list, too."

Kem's eyes were beyond depth. "Do you know, it is not good for my spirit, but I believe I enjoy being with you."

Durell joined Kem at the little temple. There were many white-robed *chees,* Buddhist nuns, attending to the women here, coming and going through ornately carved teak doors to the inner courtyard. Kem knew his way. The courtyard was crowded with people

going through the ceremonial circum-
ambulation, carrying lighted candles and
white lotus blossoms. There were graystone
Chinese pagodas and bronze horses and a
serene gilded Buddha who gazed down at the
happy, jostling worshippers.

"Wait here," said Kem. "I will find the
abbot."

The monk was not gone for long. When
he returned, he simply nodded and they
walked back to the canal.

"I have been granted a pilgrimage to the
Wat Siddha Thai," said Kem. "It is up near
the northeastern border."

"For how long?"

"Time is of no importance. Where is the
old man?"

The sampan was empty. It rocked a little
on the brown canal water, in the wake of a
passing rice barge. Durell was not surprised
that the sampan-man was gone.

"Mr. Chuk has a fine organization," he
said quietly. "There are eyes watching me
everywhere."

"What shall we do? There are no buses
from here to the airport you want," Kem
said.

"We'll take the sampan ourselves."

"But that would be stealing," Kem
objected mildly. "He is only a poor old man,

trying to earn a few dishonest *bahts* by informing of your whereabouts, am I not right?"

"Let's call it borrowing," Durell said, "if it eases your conscience, Flivver."

The monk smiled. "Yes. Very well. This will be like old times, I see."

By nine o'clock the city was behind them. The canal meandered alongside a levee, where a road had been built and above them they occasionally saw a wooden mosquito bus go by, leaving a plume of red dust in the hot, motionless air. The water was muddy and stagnant against a background of broad delta rice fields and occasional jungled growth of tall *takhien* trees. Here and there a temple sparkled in the morning sun amid teakwood farmhouses that stood drunkenly on weary stilts. From one of the farmhouses that snuggled under tall palm trees came rock-and-roll radio music, and two young Thai girls roared by on the parallel road, casually astride their Honda. There were flowering shrubs in the farmyard, a vegetable garden, papaya and banana trees, clumps of bamboo. A line of monks from the local *wat* trudged across the field with their alms bowls and gift packets. Two brightly colored kites flew in the brazen sky.

"In the Sangha," said Kem, "there are

115

227 Rules of Conduct, Sam. There are prohibitions against sex, lying, stealing and alcohol. It is easy to leave the Brotherhood, by simply stating it is one's wish. Will you force me to do so?"

"Don't worry about it, Flivver. How far are we from Lung Moc?"

The monk raised his arm and pointed across the hot delta fields. "It is just over there."

The time was nine-thirty in the morning.

Benjie was waiting on the dusty little airstrip outside the village. There was a haze in the air to the south, over Bangkok. Her Thai Star twin-engined Apache, with its broad red stripe down the fuselage, was ready. The girl's hands were stained with grease, and there was a smudge on her left cheek. But her green eyes were clear and relieved when Durell showed up from the canal side with Kem silently at his side.

"Who is that?" she asked suspiciously.

"Brother Kem Pasah Borovit. Otherwise known as Flivver. He comes with us."

"Don't tell me he's another of your spooks?"

"Yes he is."

Benjie shook her head. She wore dusty yellow slacks and a blue shirt and carried a

116

leather flying jacket over her arm. A battered flight bag was already in the open luggage compartment of the plane. She wore sunglasses pushed up on top of her head, tangled in her red-gold hair, which was still done up in a prim knot. Durell tried to picture her with her hair down, but it was impossible. Benjie's image was too firmly fixed in his mind. He turned to Kem.

"Did you take care of the sampan?"

"I sank it. The old man will not find it, and know where we have gone. It is a sin. I fear my spirit will lose much merit in the coming days."

Benjie said, "Are you one of those fighting monks I've read about?"

"I am a brother of the Sangha. I do what I think is best under the benevolent eye of heaven."

Benjie stared at the man without eyebrows and hair. "You give me the creeps," she said flatly.

"You are not an object of beauty to me, either," said Kem mildly. "But since we are both obligated to assist *Nai* Durell, we should try to maintain a pleasant relationship."

Benjie looked at Durell. "Do we really need him?"

"We do."

The girl shrugged. "Well, let's go, before the cops catch up to us."

14

At four in the afternoon, the Apache came down to a delicate landing on a strip of field at the logging camp, cut like a narrow ribbon through the dense forest south-east of Chiengmai. During the flight, Durell monitored the radio, while Kem sat in the back. He heard nothing alarming from Bangkok, now safely hundreds of miles to the south.

A mountain breeze blew through the wide, rolling valley, where a shallow river meandered quietly. The dark green of the teak woods was a relieving contrast to the jangled brilliance of Bangkok. The wind was cool. Here and there on the mountainsides were small villages, connected by thread-like roads that followed old elephant trails. Color splashed from the frangipani trees. Their elevation was just a little less than five thousand feet.

Chiengmai, the second largest city in

Thailand, lay about fifty miles from the logging camp. The only connection was by a narrow-gauge logging railway and the dusty, sinuous mountain roads. The Slocum teak enterprise was about a quarter-mile from the landing strip, but the plane had been spotted as Benjie flew down the valley, and two battered jeeps racketed into sight as they rolled to a stop.

The momentary stillness, except for the cool, steady wind, was pleasant. Four Thai mountain men, with cloth headbands and heavy logging boots, jumped from the jeeps.

"*Chaiyo*, Miss Slocum. You surprise us!"

"We won't be here long, Nam. It depends on my friends here."

"The *bhikkhu?*" Nam looked surprised.

"No, the American."

"Of course, of course. We have heard of him." Nam laughed. "The police telephone village. Make much upset of people. Army also. Asking for big American. We say we know nothing." Nam laughed again. He was missing several front teeth, but he carried an old Sten gun that had survived from World War II, and it was carefully polished and cleaned. A bandolier of clips hung from his meaty shoulders. He was bowlegged, barefooted, and tough. "Did we do the right thing, Miss Slocum?"

119

"Exactly right." Benjie looked worriedly at Durell. "How could they know we were coming here?"

"An educated guess. General Savag isn't stupid."

"Have we much time?"

"Less than I'd hoped."

The teak logger, Nam, made a spitting sound. "General Savag? He comes here?"

"We hope not. Does he worry you?"

"Bad man. Not true Thai. We hate him." Nam shrugged. "The work goes well, Miss Slocum. We almost finished third quarter section over on Ko Dinh Bong. Two rafts almost ready for river. Old Josie – you remember her? – she very sick, but vet gets her better." Nam looked at Durell. "Old Josie a logging elephant. We have eight here."

Durell asked Nam to hide and camouflage the plane, and the bandy-legged man gave quick orders to this three helpers. Then Nam said, "Is Mr. Mike coming here, too?"

"We don't know," Benjie said.

She turned and walked abruptly toward the jeeps. Her back and shoulders looked stiff and straight.

The logging camp, which looked like a mountain tribal hamlet, was beside a rushing tributary to the river below. There were large

120

sheds for the elephants, who were out on the forest trails at this hour, and houses of woven bamboo and plaited roofs standing on stilts. The women carried Lao-type *habs,* with their hair in ornate side knots and tight, dark blue blouses with shining silver buttons that went from waist to collar. Most wore white cotton *pasins* with their blouses. There was a rundown store, a food commissary, another open shed for tools, two battered trucks, and the sawyers' machinery. The smell of cut mahogany and teak logs and wood chips fought with the scents of frangipani and the smoke from charcoal stoves in the workmen's houses. There was always the inevitable effluvium of a mountain settlement. The men in sight, like Nam the foreman, reminded Durell of Southwest American Indians, being taller than most Thai, with bandy legs and high cheekbones.

There were two larger structures, one a Western-style bungalow with a veranda, built of rough boarding, and a tiny *wat* at the far end of the single street, which followed the stream in typical linear fashion.

"You have a *bhikkhu* here?" Kem asked the foreman.

"No, father, not for several months."

"Do you wish me to perform prayers?"

"If you like, father. Will you be here long?"

Durell said, "Only overnight."

"Whatever the *bhikkhu* chooses to do will make us grateful," Nam said to Kem.

Beyond the brook and the bungalow, where Benjie headed with a long stride, were some clearings and fields planted on the terraced mountain slope, growing some rice and tobacco and bananas. Two of the fields looked as if they had been used to grow poppies. Kem asked to be excused and headed down the village street toward the small temple. Durell followed Benjie across a log bridge over the brook to the bungalow. His eye caught the glimmer of aerial wire from a radio antenna, and he traced it to the bungalow roof before he stepped up on the veranda after Benjie.

She was waiting inside, in a small den, her fists jammed on her hips. She looked angry and tired.

"All right, what now?"

"We're looking for Mike, remember?"

"You're looking for more than Mike. Tell me about it. All of it, Sam. Don't hold back, or we'll be in trouble. I can smell trouble here, already. The place doesn't feel normal, somehow. Nam talks too much. The women aren't chattering, the way they usually do.

122

I feel like a stranger here. And I practically built this camp with my own two hands and recruited the local tribesmen myself, and had them trained as loggers. They ought to be here by now, finished with their day's work. It's not like these people to put in voluntary overtime. Sam, I'm worried."

"Where's your radio transmitter?" he asked.

"What's that got to do with what I'm asking?"

"Maybe everything. Maybe we can talk to Mike."

Benjie stared at him. "You don't give much, do you? You still act as if I'm a suspect, in whatever you're looking for."

"It could be," Durell said. Then he surprised her by crossing the hot, shadowed room and kissing her on the mouth. "You're also a hell of a good pilot, Benjie."

Her lips were cold and surprised, hardening under the quick pressure of his mouth. Stepping back, he watched her eyes widen with astonishment, then reflexive anger, then something that was not quite amusement.

"And what was that for?"

"For being a woman," he said.

"I didn't think you could tell," she snapped. She drew a deep breath. "Let's see to the radio, Sam. We need something to eat, too. And we're not safe here, as I said."

"We're not safe anywhere," he replied.

Durell worked on the radio while Benjie slammed things around in the kitchen, shouted at a native woman and drove her off in a fine fit of pretended fury. Durell half hoped, as he worked on the transmitter, to hear her break into singing; but Benjie didn't go quite that far. Nevertheless, after a time, there was a pause in the kitchen, while he smelled rice and pork and sauce bubbling away, and when she returned, her face was scrubbed clean and her eyes shone and her hair was pulled back in a neat bun. He said nothing about it.

"Can you do it? Can you reach Mike?"

"If he's listening. Can you trust Nam?"

She said, "Like you, Sam, I don't trust anyone."

The radio hummed and crackled. Energy came from the camp generator that powered donkey engines and logging machinery at the other end of the village. Durell put on the earphones, and once again heard the ghost voices, the uncertain music, the ranting across the misty lost mountains of the Golden Triangle between Thailand, Burma and Laos.

But he did not hear Mike Slocum's voice.

124

Durell knew he was late making the rendezvous, but it couldn't be helped. He hadn't known about General Savag when he spoke to Mike last night. And Xo Dong was still over a hundred-mile flight east into the primitive border area.

"Sam, do you think Mike is still all right?"

He looked up from the radio. Her face was flushed. "Mike was okay, last night."

"Are you out to save him – or kill him?"

He listened to the sighing of electronic waves from the radio, heard nothing but a dim surf of discordant Asian music, and said, "It all has to do with the poppy fields out there, the ones you let your logger families grow."

"Oh, that. I can't stop them. Every village around here, all the way up into Burma and over into Laos, grows poppy. Do you think...?" She paused, her fists clenched at her sides. Her green eyes went angry. "You don't really think we're part of the Muc Tong, do you? You can't think..."

"Is the Muc Tong the smuggling syndicate?"

"Oh, you bastard," she whispered. "You cold, mean, cruel man. You kissed me, and yet you think I –"

"Answer me."

"No, Sam."

125

"You have the transport, the men, the whole system."

"No, Sam."

"You, or Mike."

"No!"

"But you know something about it."

Her face was white. "Just the local stuff. What's happening around here. They put some pressure on us, about a month ago, to use our logging rafts going down the Ping River toward Bangkok. They wanted us to take on their men – hoodlums, mountain riffraff, some Chinese overseers, to transport heroin from a refinery about twenty miles northeast of this valley. It's a big set-up, sure. But you can't believe that I'd lend the Thai Star business facilities...?"

"Why not?" he asked. "And if not you, why not Mike?"

"But you're his friend!" she cried.

He shook his head. "Not if he's guilty. Not if he uses your business to take money from the Muc Tong to line his own pockets. Maybe you're innocent, but maybe Mike is not. He could be calling me into a trap, because I've got a thread or two of the network in my hands. To him, if he's in it, I'm an immediate and obvious danger."

"Call him," she said desperately. "I want to talk to him."

126

"Xo Dong doesn't answer."

"I'll prove to you –"

"We'll prove it together. I need you, Benjie, and I need Kem to get me into the mountains without every tribesman trying to cut off my head. Since Mike doesn't answer, he might be dead. I'm trying to be honest with you." He turned off the radio. "When the Muc Tong came to you, did they just want your rafts, or did they want the planes, too?"

"The whole thing – and my ships, too. I told them to go to hell."

"Who approached you?"

"A very slick, smooth character, at the sawmill."

"One of Chuk's men?"

"I don't know. No, not Chuk's hoodlums. Somebody above Chuk. Not the Chinese who led the sawyers last night, either. But someone like him." She shook her head, her eyes still appalled. "When I refused to have anything to do with them I was threatened with strikes, fire, and sabotage."

"You think last night was part of it?"

"Oh, sure," she said wearily. "It's been going on for months. If it keeps up, I'll be wiped out."

"That's a good sign," Durell said. "If

127

Mike threw in with them, they'd have stopped harassing you."

"Thanks for nothing," she said bitterly.

Durell turned abruptly. From over the rolling hills came faint popping noises, a dim shouting, thin as a whisper in the distance. He turned, strode out on the bungalow veranda. Long evening shadows lay on the valley. Several of the village women stood very still, looking up through the surrounding teak forest toward the mountain peak. The foreman, Nam, came out of the machine shed and also stared.

Benjie whispered, "It's gunfire."

"Speak of the devil. The Muc Tong?"

"They've raided the logging crews before. Maybe they know I've just arrived. The men won't work for a week, now."

"Have you any rifles?"

She turned and ran into the bungalow and came out with two Remington .30-30's. Nam, the foreman, had gotten into a jeep and came bouncing toward them, raising plumes of red dust in the evening air. The breeze felt suddenly colder. Durell checked the magazines of the rifles and waved Nam down.

"It is trouble, Miss Benjie!"

"I know. The elephants." She turned to Durell to explain. "We're logging a strip

128

where we can't jeep in. Only the elephants can do the work. If the Muc Tong kill them, we're done for – they're too expensive to replace and train."

The logging road led uphill, following the white rushing stream. Above the racket of the engine, they heard more distant gunfire, and then an explosion, as if a grenade had been thrown. Men screamed up there, in the dense green of the forest; but the stately, towering trees made an umbrella over the sky and screened off the camp and the cutting site.

Teak was durable, lasting for centuries, and was not a prey to tropical termites. It was never cut until it was at least two feet in diameter, or about 150 years old. The logging method usually followed girdling to kill the tree, which was then left standing for two years to dry out, to lighten the density of the wood and permit it to float. Elephants were used to fell the trees, most often in the rainy season when the timber did not split easily; but obviously Benjie had been pushing her loggers to work now, even when it was dry. After the loggers trimmed the logs, the massive elephants, using chains guided by their mahouts, dragged the logs either to trucks or a narrow-gauge railroad for the trip over the mountainside to the nearest usable stream, where rafts were made up and regular watch-stations were erected to permit men and elephants to loosen any jams. Where the stream widened, rafts were constructed of the logs, using two or three hundred of them, and tower-huts for the crew, with rudders fore and aft, were set up for the year-long trip down to the delta sawmills.

Durell's thoughts were abruptly interrupted by a glimpse of running men through the tall trees. The path twisted sharply to the right, and Nam suddenly screamed. Directly before them stood a huge gray mass, with tiny, anger-reddened eyes.

It was one of the logging elephants. A broken chain from one foreleg whipped like a vicious, incredible weapon through the air as the ponderous, terrified beast charged toward them. Blood ran down its side from several bullet wounds.

Nam yelled and abandoned the wheel and jumped free. The jeep hit a rut in the dirt road and bounced, lifting on the right side, and came down with a bone-rattling crash. Durell grabbed at the wheel, but it tore out of his hands.

The huge beast, maddened by its wounds, was only fifty feet away. Benjie called out something from the back of the jeep as the elephant thundered down on them.

130

Durell got his foot on the brake, caught the wheel again, and turned the jeep into the brush. It was almost stopped when Nam, shrieking, ran ahead with arms outstretched, directly in the elephant's path. The ground shook with the beast's charge.

There were only moments to spare when Durell grabbed at Benjie and rolled out of the jeep with her into the underbrush beside the trail. At the same moment, the elephant reached Nam. The foreman was still shrieking the animal's name when the broken foot-chain swung at him from the ponderous front feet. The chain literally tore Nam's head from his body.

The elephant thundered by. One leg caught the jeep and there was a crash of metal and a shattering of glass and the jeep rocked and turned over, tumbling down the slope of the mountainside through the trees.

"Nam . . ." Benjie moaned.

"Don't look at him," Durell snapped.

The animal was safely past when he regained the jeep and grabbed one of the rifles. If the beast reached the village, with those murderous foot-chains, there would be little left of either houses or women. Fortunately, the elephant paused. Blood poured from the wounds in its side. The trunk swung this way and that, the small ears

131

of its Asian ancestry flapped forward. It was aware of Benjie and Durell now, and it turned, small eyes glaring at them. The jeep had crashed into a tree and halted. Slowly, the elephant completed its turn and began to move toward them.

"Wait, he's too valuable –" Benjie began.

"So was Nam."

"He fired, twice, three times. The animal kept coming. He fired a fourth time and the beast stumbled, went to its front knees, and suddenly tumbled over with a thud that shook the ground again.

There was a long silence, interlaced by the sigh of the evening wind in the tall teak trees.

Benjie swore softly.

"Come along," Durell said.

He carried the rifle in the crook of his arm and started up the trail, not looking back to see if Benjie followed. He passed the bloody mess that remained of the Thai foreman without looking at it twice. Up ahead, he heard the sounds of men and a truck engine, but there were no more shots.

Presently, Benjie caught up with him.

"Sam, wait. I'm sorry about Nam and the elephant."

"Enter it in red ink in your ledgers," he snapped.

A truck filled with men came down the

trail. Some wore bloody rags to bandage their wounds. Another truck, a flat-bed, carried their logging tools. Behind them, in a long line, came five work elephants, their massive gray bodies swaying as they walked. The mahouts treated them very gingerly.

The whole procession halted when they saw Durell and Benjie in their way.

15

The raid by the Muc Tong was one of several in the past month, the new headman explained. He was a tall, bony tribesman with grizzled gray hair and a frightened grin. "We drove them off, Miss Benjie. We kill two, we think."

"And our people?" she asked thinly.

"We lose five. And poor Nam."

"And the equipment?"

"They took saws. We must get more, from the supply at Chiengmai."

It took some time to remove the elephant's carcass from the road, using logging winches on the trucks. Some of the men gathered Nam's remains in a blanket, and put the corpse in the second truck. They were silent

and dispirited. Benjie tried to raise their morale, then gave up. The women in the village wailed as the little procession came into camp.

"When the government hears of it," she said tightly, "they'll put it down as a terrorist raid, from the insurgents. But it was the Muc Tong, all right. The opium smugglers. So far I've held out against them, refused my facilities, but I think I'm finished here. The logging won't go on for another month. I'll lose Rafts Five and Six, this way. There won't be enough material for the Bangkok mill, next year."

The village was silent as the sun went down, but the women did the cooking. Durell and Benjie ate Thai noodles and Chinese fried rice and some pork. He drank a bottle of icy beer from Benjie's refrigerator in the bungalow. Benjie offered him some whiskey, but he shook his head.

"We have to go on," he said.

"But I hate to leave the camp now, in such a mess."

"Do you have any dynamite here?"

"What do you want dynamite for?"

"Mike asked for it. I don't know why."

"He didn't radio. He can't be alive now."

The girl's straight shoulders were slumped, and she scarcely touched their
134

makeshift meal. He wondered how much of her low spirits came from her financial loss, and how much was sorrow for the trials of the people she employed here. The sound of mourning bells came from the little temple down the village street. A woman's voice keened through the evening mist. The heavy thud of a restless elephant echoed from the big sheds at the other end of the camp.

Durell said quietly, "Benjie, I think Mike can hold out until we get to him. I don't know if he's using Thai Star transport systems to help the Muc Tong smugglers. Maybe he's been blackmailed into it. Or maybe the whole thing is a trap set to get me to the Xo Dong area, where I can be taken – a price Mike might have agreed to pay. In this business, you can't count on anything or anyone. My job is to hamper, damage, or stop the big syndicate that's been formed to transport, refine and distribute drugs. Turkey, as a source of opium, is being dried up. The Golden Triangle here is taking shape as the next biggest supplier to American troops and our youngsters at home. Somebody is at the head of it. I think of it as a dragon, and my job is to cut off the dragon's head."

"Mike isn't capable of running anything as big as that," the girl said quietly.

135

A rolling white mist filled the valley over the river, covering the distant mountains with a milky light. The wind made the temple bells sound louder. A baby wailed somewhere in the village. Dogs barked. The dull thud of the diesel generator made a rhythmic sound that wove through the camp in a steady, monotonous pattern.

Benjie's green eyes were as shrouded as the foggy mountain valley. "But you think *I* have the ability to be the dragon head, right? I'm a smart busineswoman, I've been driven all my life to take care of Mike, to succeed, to do what my parents never managed to do. Do you know what our childhood was like, Sam? Mike and I never had a real home. We never stayed in one place long enough to really learn anything, in school, or to make childhood friends. What we know now, we got from reading, from studying together, whenever we could. Our father was a drunk and our mother was just as irresponsible. They could barely take care of themselves, much less two kids. Can you imagine? When they were both killed in a car crash, I had to take care of Mike, even though I'm only two years older than he. And Mike is like my father. Reckless, charming, and totally irresponsible. So I worked. I educated him. I made a home for him. And when the chance came to build up something solid and decent and profitable in Thailand, so we'd never, never have to worry about money again, I took it. I worked hard. I've done what I set out to do. Maybe I've passed up a lot in life that I could have had, instead. But do you honestly think I'd risk everything I've won, by committing some stupid, criminal act? Not blackmail, not the worst sort of pressure from Chuk and the people behind him, could make me do it."

"But suppose it was to save Mike?" Durell asked.

"I've thought about that. Everything I did was for him, and I just don't know what I'd do, in that case. But I still don't think I'd throw away Thai Star. Not even for Mike, now." She made a rueful mouth. "That's how far I've come from being a normal woman," she said sadly. "Why did you kiss me, Sam?"

"You simply looked right for it."

"Ha. I'm not all that attractive. I know what I usually look like, sloppy in slacks and junk. I'm always too busy to go shopping. I've never learned to have fun buying dresses and cosmetics and things like that. There never was enough time, you see. There were always more important things to do. So why did you kiss me?"

"Did it bother you?"

Her green eyes slid aside. "I – I liked it."

"God. Don't make an issue out of it."

"But I *liked* it, Sam. You – you're different."

"How many men have kissed you, Benjamina?"

She flushed. "That's not fair."

"How many?"

"Very few." She shivered, then stood up to gather the dinner dishes and took them into the kitchen, and she was gone for several minutes. She looked as if she had been crying when she came back, and she had washed her face and pulled back her hair more neatly. She had a tall, proud body.

"All right, Sam. What do you want me to do?"

"We need the dynamite for Mike, assuming he's still alive, and assuming it's not a trap. We'll need other supplies, bottled water, some food, maybe, and your plane, of course. How long does it take to get to Chiengmai? We can't fly there. General Savag's people would pick us up in no time. We'd have to go by mountain road."

"Make it two hours," she said.

"Then let's get Kem, and go. You say you have a supply place in Chiengmai?"

"Oh, yes."

Smiling, he pulled her to him and kissed her again. She reacted differently, this time. Her hand came up and she slapped him hard, her arm strong, the blow stinging. Her eyes flashed with resentment.

"You –" she paused, breathing angrily, "don't play games with me, Cajun. Remember that."

16

The girls of Chiengmai were small and pert, with slim bodies and dark eyes, and they looked jaunty in their bright, Western clothes as they walked together down Tu Duong Road. Benjie stopped the jeep in front of a long hotel with a bright yellow exterior, not far from a bridge over the shallow Ping River. Two sloe-eyed Indian ladies in saris led their paunchy businessmen husbands into the lobby ahead of them. An old clock over the desk, half-hidden by potted palms, read ten o'clock. The night was hot. With Kem bouncing in the rear of the jeep, they

139

had covered the mountain road from the logging camp in less than three hours.

"I always stay here," Benjie said. "We need a place to wash up and rest for a few hours, until I get the dynamite and other things. The Third Army runs air patrols toward Xo Dong, and it would be helpful if I can learn their schedule. And we can't very well hang about on the streets, can we?"

"I wish," said Kem mildly, "to go to the Wat Kala Prem, to see an old friend."

"Can you get the dynamite alone, Benjie?" Durell asked.

"No problem. I have keys to our warehouse."

Durell turned to the monk. "I'll go with you, Flivver."

The monk looked slantwise at him. "It is purely a religious matter, Sam. But perhaps we can help you, too. In this city there are many Westerners, but in the Xo Dong area you would be too obvious. One glimpse of you by a hostile villager, and the alarm would go to the Muc Tong as well as to General Savag. But perhaps I can make you less conspicuous. It will not take long. Also, I may be able to learn something from the *bhikkhus* about the opium smuggling. You would be surprised at what the the Sangha knows. Xo Dong was settled mostly by

140

North Vietnamese, you know. They fled here, many centuries ago, from the Chinese emperors. I believe they are still loyal to Hanoi, so it is dangerous country for you. These *yuan* – the emigré Vietnamese – go easily across the border into Laos and across to North Vietnam. As easily as the Muc Tong."

There were few U.S. military men on Chiengmai's streets, although the city had been designated as a strategic military base. Here and there in the crowded lanes were distinctively dressed hill people of the Miao, Lissu and Yao tribes. Bicycle traffic whirled among the autos and buses, and the Thai spoken here was faintly touched with Lao dialect. Many of the shops were still open at this hour of the night. The streets were brightly lighted near the hotel, but then became narrow alleys of the old city, the former capital of ancient empires. Bells tinkled, noodle stalls gave off their tantalizing aromas, and there was a steady underbeat of clip-clopping wooden sandals. Kem walked with a long stride, leading the way with familiarity. There were neon-lighted cinemas and cafes, discotheques, avant-garde art galleries side by side with old dusty shops exhibiting Sukhothai art and topaz and zircon gems.

"Wait," said Durell.

Kem stopped. "What is it?"

They were near the great Chiengmai monastery of Wat Phra Sihing. The chanting of monks, the chattering of women passing by, and the rattle of motorcycles did not make Durell stir. He watched a long military limousine sweep by under the light of the street lamps.

"What is it?" the *bhikkhu* asked again.

Durell watched the big car vanish in the traffic. "Miss Ku Tu Thiet, with General Savag. That's twice I've seen him near me, in a car. Cozy as can be, with the girl."

"What does it mean?"

"You go on," Durell decided. "Wait for me on the other side of the wat."

"There is danger?"

"Plenty of it. Go on."

Durell dodged a flood of bicycles released by the traffic light as he crossed the street. Kem vanished in the nighttime throngs near the monastery. A pair of giggling Thai girls in pink *pasabais* approached and said something. He ignored them. He saw no one suspicious in the street. But instinct made him wary. He walked faster, then paused in front of the jewelery shop again. A dog inside the shop barked at him. He saw two men risk their lives, as he had done, crossing the heavy

142

traffic. They wore Western clothes and straw hats. They could have been twins. Durell turned the corner into a side street. The towering *prangs* and *chedis* of the Wat Phra Sihing kept him oriented in the twisting alleys. The two men followed him into the narrow lanes, hurrying past dim shops that sold ornaments and religious articles. An ice cream vendor shouted his wares at him. A man with a Cambodian gibbon on his shoulder offered it for sale. Durell halted near some women with *habs* on their shoulders, the sticks weighted down with two balanced baskets loaded with vegetables.

"Sir? Durell?"

One of the men in the straw hats shouted at him over the heads of the two women. Durell dodged aside from a bullock cart that all but blocked the narrow street and walked fast, back toward the wat. He did not know if the men were Savag's or from the Muc Tong. Maybe it was all one and the same. Mike Slocum had the answers, somewhere in the mountains to the north. Maybe coming into Chiengmai was a mistake; maybe the dynamite wasn't important. Maybe Benjie had spent the time sending the two goons after him.

He shook the questions from his mind. The straw hats were as persistent as flies. He could see the throngs of worshipers near the wat again, the crowd accented by the saffron robes of several hundred monks. Some sort of religious festival was being celebrated.

The straw hats had closed the gap. Their brown faces were ugly. One had his hand inside his jacket.

"This way, mister."

A teen-aged Thai boy in the robe of a *dek wat* tugged at his sleeve. Durell roughly shrugged him off. The boy persisted. "No worry. Holy Kem sends me. Bad men be lost." A small swirl of worshipers intervened between Durell and his pursuers for a moment. The boy said, "In here, sir."

It was a musty apothecary shop, devoted to Chinese herbs, pickled snakes, strange jars filled with muddy-colored powders. The proprietor bobbed his head and ducked out of the way. The boy led Durell to the rear. The two men in straw hats were on the sidewalk outside, and the lighted street cast their shadows against the cluttered, fly-specked window.

"All right," said Durell. "Lead on."

They ducked behind a fringed curtain in the rear. The Chinese apothecary chattered something in Cantonese, but Durell did not look back. The rear door gave on an alley, hard by the monastery. He heard the deep-throated clang of bronze bells, the tinkle of silver ones, the heavy chanting of priests; he smelled incense, the odor of food offerings. The alley was backed on the other side by two and three-story wooden houses, decked with verandas, poles with paper lanterns agleam, and a teeming huddle of tenement dwellers. Durell felt tall and conspicuous among them as he went up rickety wooden steps, through a bedroom where a startled woman sat upright with a sigh of surprise. The *dek wat* grinned and said, "My mama."

From the alley came angry shouting. The woman did not get up from the bed. There was a single, tin-shaded electric light in the room, casting deep shadows.

"Come. My papa."

The man in the other room was thin and brown, wearing a striped lavender shirt, khaki slacks, and sneakers. He sat at a porcelain-topped table next to a large cooking stove. The overhead light cast deep shadows on his face. He did not smile. He was busy laying out pots and jars and bits of theatrical hair on a newspaper spread on the table, and something bubbled on the stove.

"Where is Kem?" Durell asked.

"He comes. My papa helps in the wat – he helps the priests in ceremonies. He also

145

works for Chin Lee theater on Hapagongwe Road. He is genius," said the boy.

The father looked dour. Durell listened for more sounds from the alley, but the shouting had ended. The Thai looked at him with grave eyes. "Sit," he said. "I make you look like Northern man. Part Chinese, maybe. I study your face."

"I haven't much time."

"I do not take long. Twenty minutes."

Durell looked around the small, hot room. The boy hovered near the door, grinning happily. The father kept working with his pots of pigments and creams and wads of coarse black hair. Durell wondered if he'd been mistaken in the single glimpse he'd had of Miss Ku in General Savag's car. Then, amid the primitive clutter of the tenement kitchen, his eye caught on an anachronism. A black telephone stood among the painted, peasant pots on the kitchen shelf.

He stood up quietly. The father lifted thick brows and pointed with a silky paint brush. "You sit. I am ready."

"Where did you get the telephone?"

"It belongs monastery. I work for *bhikkhus*. They need me, they telephone." The man smiled for the first time. "Very modern, up-to-date, first class. Gives me much importance."

146

"Can you call anyone in the city?"

"No."

The boy said, "My father means he has no other friends in Chiengmai who own telephones, so he can't call anyone but the abbot or the monks in the wat."

"But it's connected to the regular system?"

"Oh, yes, sir. You wish to use? Please do so."

Durell tested the black telephone. There was a humming in his ear. He heard more noises from the street growing louder again. The two straw hats out there were getting frustrated. All at once the telephone clicked and a woman spoke in Thai, asking what number he wished to call.

He gave James D. James' number in Bangkok.

The operator was appalled. "It is long distance, very expensive."

"I'll pay," Durell said.

"You not Thai. You not speak good Thai," the woman said in English.

"Just get me the number."

It was a risk, of course. He did not know how far-reaching was either Savag's intelligence system or the Muc Tong's. Nor did he know if James' phone was being tapped.

147

The father of the temple boy got up and began to apply pigment to his white face while he waited at the telephone for the connection to go through. He heard a sing-song radio playing in the next apartment, another radio blasting Western soul music. There was shouting and argument in the alley. Kem did not appear. The telephone seemed to have gone dead. He felt the brownish makeup going on his face, in his ears and down his throat and across the back of his neck. The telephone crackled and then he heard a distant ringing. He wondered if there would be trouble for the make-up man and the young temple boy. If the call were traced by the Muc Tong or Savag, it might also uncover Kem as a sleeper agent put on active duty. But there was no help for it. He wouldn't have come to Chiengmai at all, if not for Mike's urgent plea for explosives. The odds in the gamble were not too favorable, Durell thought

"Hallo?"

Suddenly Jimmy James' voice was in his ear. The make-up man added hair to Durell's eyebrows with spirit gum.

Durell said, "Red Fish here. I'm on my way to Brooklyn Omega."

There was a long pause. Then, "Is your phone secure?"

148

"No."

"Then hang up."

"I need some answers."

"Then I'll hang up," James said flatly.

"Are you being bugged?"

"I've been questioned. You're ordered out of the country. Understand? They're on to you, they're out to get you. I'll send someone else in after Mike."

"It will be too late by then," Durell said. "Is Miss Ku there?"

"What?"

"Your little helper."

"Yes, of course she's here. Why?"

"Put her on the telephone," Durell said.

"Well, she's not actually in the house. But I expect her back any moment. Look here, old boy, I don't know what you're doing, you should be at your destination right now. Where are you?"

"When did you last see Miss Ku?"

"A few hours ago." James' voice sharpened with irritation, anxiety – perhaps fear. "Why are you interested?"

"I just saw her in Chiengmai with General Savag."

"She's in Bangkok. I tell you, she'll be back any moment. We have a supper party planned for some Embassy people. She acts as my hostess, since I'm a bachelor."

149

"Are you sure she's in Bangkok?"

"I'd stake my life on it."

"You may have to," Durell said, and hung up.

17

"You look fine," Kem said. "Tall, of course, but you can pass for a Chinese mixture anywhere up here. A man from Yunnan, perhaps, with Russian blood? No problem, Sam," Kem paused. "At the temple, I inquired about the Muc Tong. The Sangha brothers were very helpful. But come, we must go."

"What shall I pay the make-up man?"

"Nothing. He makes *tam boon* – much merit – by helping the *bhikkhus*. He will say nothing. In any case, he is an *acharn*, a wizard, and the people are still superstitious and believe in *phis*, spirits, and wizardry. They will not bother an *acharn*."

They left the tenement by way of the rickety stairs to the alley. Two solid-looking men sat on the bottom steps, as if on guard, and they jumped up respectfully as Kem led

150

the way. There was no sign of the two men in straw hats.

"I wish we could take a *samlaw*," Kem said, "but it would not look right for a *bhikku* to ride that way." He bobbed his bald head. "We must walk back to the hotel, but not to fast. I wish to meditate."

"Flivver," Durell said, "I don't doubt your sincerity, but we have work to do."

"I do the Lord Buddha's work," said the monk. His black eyes twinkled. "But sometimes the way is most mysterious."

As they walked back to meet Benjie, Kem told him that the Muc Tong was everywhere. An alert had gone out for a tall American – Durell, obviously. There was also a police alarm throughout the city. Kem did not know if it was military or civil police. In the dark makeup and bushy brows put on by the *acharn*, Durell felt as if any of the hundreds of night passersby could see through the fraud. But no one looked at him twice. Now and then a woman gave Kem a quick *wai*, a smile, and hurried past. A police car hooted by, but did not slow or give the monk and the tall Chinese their attention.

Benjie, waiting nervously in the hotel room, was startled by Durell's appearance. "Lordie, you've changed over for sure,

151

Cajun. It's a good job. There are plenty of mixes like you up in the mountains."

"Did you get the dynamite?"

"It's in the jeep, behind the hotel. But I think some security people followed me here. I'm nervous."

"We'll go out the back way."

The jeep was parked in deep shadow under slender palm trees. The explosives were in a small wooden box in the back. Durell pried it open and examined the sticks and the detonator and battery quickly. Everything seemed in order.

"I hope it's enough," Benjie said. She looked pale and wan in the gloomy shadows behind the hotel.

"It will have to do."

The exit from the parking lot came out on the main street fronting the hotel. Bicycles and cars flowed by in a steady stream. Lights shone in most of the back windows of the hotel, but some of the bamboo shades were drawn. The sweeping overhang of the Thai roof kept the upper windows in shadow. He couldn't tell if anyone watched them from up there, or not. The jeep, easily identified as Benjie's, could trap them on the road back to the logging camp. Benjie and Kem were also uncertain. Durell walked into the shadows of the lot to examine an old flat-bodied truck parked near the kitchen entrance. The kitchen was closed and dark at this hour. The truck was empty.

Kem stood beside him. "We must not steal it, Sam."

"The jeep is dangerous," Durell said.

"I would not sin against the Way of the Sangha."

"We're fighting an evil thing, Flivver."

"True. Perhaps I can rationalize the move. I agree about the jeep. I'll get the dynamite."

The truck was an old rattletrap, with a simple ignition system that Durell shorted in a moment. Kem brought the explosives and Benjie helped him stow it on the floor of the cab. The wheel felt greasy and the cab smelled of old sweat and stale food. The gas tank looked to be half full – just about enough to get them the fifty miles back to the logging camp and the plane.

The engine started with a fearful racket that echoed back from the walls of the hotel; but no one came yelling as Durell backed and then turned toward the exit and the traffic on the boulevard. He thought he glimpsed the two straw hats again, near the lobby entrance. For a moment he was sure they had spotted him, but their eyes passed over him without interest.

153

In twenty minutes they were on the road heading east into the mountains again, leaving Chiengmai behind.

18

At midnight, they arrived at the camp. It was deserted. The elephants were gone, the sheds were empty, and fire had burned down the machinery shack. The embers still smoldered, a dark and evil glow in the black night. A warm wind blew up the valley and made the charred beams flicker and spark. The racket of the truck's engine echoed back and forth from the black mountainsides, and Durell shut off the engine some distance from the camp, the moment he spotted the fires.

"Oh, God," Benjie murmured. "I'm cleaned out."

"All the people have gone," said Kem. "I pity them."

Durell said, "The Muc Tong may still be around."

He got out and listened to the wind in the black forest around them. The trail ahead was empty. From what he could see of the main street, only a single lost dog ambled about, sniffing at the ruins and under the stilted houses.

The bungalow across the creek had been burned down.

"The plane?" Durell said.

Benjie's face was pale. "Maybe they missed it. The airstrip is a bit away from the village, remember. Do you still think I've got a hand in the Muc Tong, Sam?"

He didn't reply. He probed the ruined village without seeing anything except the dog that now trotted away into the brush, holding something in its jaws. He started the engine again. "They were here an hour ago, at least."

"Is it not a risk to drive through?" Kem asked mildly. "We make a good target."

"Better than on foot," Durell said.

He forced the old vehicle into gear and tramped on the worn gas pedal. The truck creaked and rolled forward, into the main street. He drove faster, dust rolling up into the blackness behind them. In the glow of the dying fires he now saw two or three bodies, sprawled in front of different houses. Benjie sucked in her breath, but said nothing. Their headlights flared and touched on the pitiful wreckage of the logging compound. Momentarily, Durell expected a hail of bullets from the shadows; but nothing happened. They were through the village in less than a minute, and bounced recklessly down the jeep trail to the landing strip. The stench of burning oil and exploded grenades still lingered in the air. The trees blocked out the valley from for moments, and then Durell saw the glimmer of the river, silvery in the starlight. In another minute they came out of the woods and roared onto the landing strip cleared on the shelf of the mountainside.

The Apache was still there. The Muc Tong had missed it.

At dawn, they were over the Golden Triangle. The folded mountains of shale, schist and limestone, with intrusive granitic caves, were just turning from black to dark green as the sun touched the eastern slopes with bright gold. Once they were buzzed by a Phantom F-4-E, and Durell did not know if it carried the U.S. emblem or the Thai Royal Air Force insignia. Benjie had dodged the screaming plane by dropping the little Apache into a sickening dive, and then she flew through dark valleys with the loom of the mountains on either side, seeming to touch their wingtips. The jet had thundered up and circled and buzzed them again. Benjie bit her lip and leaned forward, holding the controls lightly in her fingertips. A mountain slope rushed at them and she banked steeply, the engines protesting, and they flew even lower down another valley, above a small river that glimmered in the starlight, and guided them for a few moments.

Kem murmured some Buddhist prayers as Benjie tipped the wings this way and that, flying low over the meandering river with the steep mountains all around them. When they came up again, just above the treetops, the Phantom was gone, its thunder fading away to the west.

"Xo Dong," Benjie said now.

She pointed north. The dawn light touched the forested slopes, the granite cliffs, a few cultivated fields where a few tribal peasants were gathering at dawn to work the tobacco, tea or poppy plots. Far to the north, a road wandered toward the borders of Burma and Laos. The village was a thin row of stilted, thatched houses on a branch of the road, below a series of broad terraces planted with tea.

"My place," Benjie said. "The one I bought from the discouraged Frenchman. It made a profit of ten, twelve thousand a year for a while. Then I had to give it up when the insurgents scared off the workers."

She flew lower, between two heavy

shoulders of the mountain that gave Durell a glimpse of a broader river that twisted sinuously to the south. The sun came up over the eastern folds of the mountains with a flare of gold, and the sky turned from black to orange and blue.

"Are you sure we can land here?" Kem asked anxiously.

"There's the strip, *bhikkhu*, " she said.

It was an overgrown clearing cut from the tangled foliage above the terraces of the tea plantation. Long, thatched drying sheds flanked one end of the small field. Durell searched the ground carefully, but saw nothing human stirring down there. As they flew lower, he noted that the roofs of the drying sheds had tumbled in, and an air of decay hung over the whole area.

Benjie bit her lip again. "Everything I've ever worked for is going to pot. I'll be broke in six months, if this keeps up. And now with Chuk threatening me about the bank loans – I don't know what I'll do. And you – with your ideas about Mike and me . . ."

"You have the motive," Durell said. "It's easy money, and you need money desperately."

"I'll manage," she snapped. "And without the Muc Tong or you."

The wheels touched. The plane bounced,

158

then the girl steadied it and they ran down the length of the clearing toward the sagging drying sheds. The air here was cooler than in Chiengmai. The dawn sky was clear and bright as Benjie rolled the Apache to a halt.

"We'll hide the plane in the sheds," Durell suggested.

They worked quickly, hurried by the light of the morning. All around them, the mountains sighed with the dawn wind. From far off, a plume of dust lifted off the Thai military road to the border. A blue haze of smoke came from over the mountain spur where they had landed, but Durell could not spot its origin. Benjie took a pack from the luggage compartment of the plane and said thinly, "Breakfast. A Thermos of tea and sandwiches. Okay?"

"Fine," Durell said. "I'd like your binoculars."

She looked at the vehicular traffic on the distant road. "That's Third Army security patrol. They waste their time. All the business is here in the hills, and they're careful not to interfere. The insurgents are here, all around us. That's why I had to give up this place. It's falling apart."

She pointed through the weed-grown terraces, where a large teak bungalow overlooked the tea plants. Everything was desolate. The main house had been fire-bombed, and stood in gutted black ruins. No one was in sight. Nothing stirred.

"Who uses those fields over the valley?" Durell asked.

"Laao tribesmen, poppy growers. The plants have just been harvested."

"And taken where?"

"Mike will know if he's alive. If we find him."

They ate quickly in the cool shelter of the drying shed, beside the plane. Kem bared one shoulder of his saffron robe and murmured prayers, his black eyes opaque, seeing nothing of the present world while he drank his tea noisily from a small bowl he fished out from under his robe. Finally he said,

"Sam, I've been here before, on a small pilgrimage, last year. It is a bad place. The Communists are everywhere. Of course, these hill people are alienated from Bangkok, since the Thai consider themselves superior to them. They will be hostile to us. Please stay close to me. They will not offer harm to me or to anyone with me, I think."

"The rebels have no respect for *bhikkhus*," Benjie snapped. "You monks have had trouble with them before."

"But I have friends here."

Xo Dong was over in the next valley. There was no way to get there except by walking. Durell took the dynamite pack, strapped to his back, Kem carried the batteries, and Benjie had her haversack. The trail was narrow and tortuous, following the natural slope of the mountain. In twenty minutes, they were sweating in the lee of the mountain, cut off from the morning breeze, and the sky took on the hue of copper. The trail had been used by oxen, and once Durell paused to examine the droppings.

"There's still traffic along here," he said.

"It's the opium growers," Benjie said. "You'd think they'd also keep up the tea plants, though."

"More money in poppies, I imagine."

The trail dipped down sharply and they heard the trickle of a mountain stream ahead, and then Durell saw a relatively new military sign nailed to a tree.

" '*Yoodt,* ' " he read. "It means, 'Stop.' "

But no one was in sight, and they walked down to a rope bridge over the stream. Another sign greeted them.

" '*Ham,* ' " he read again. " 'Forbidden.' Were these here before, Benjie?"

"No. But I haven't been here for over a year."

161

"It's signed by General Uva Savag, right? So we're within his military jurisdiction."

"Yes."

They crossed the bridge without being challenged. The rutted trail came out of the woods and skirted several cultivated plots where tobacco and bananas were being grown. Normally, there would be women in their lampshade hats, weeding the soil, while children tumbled with the patient bullocks. But again, no one was in sight. A house at the far end of the field was empty; the charcoal stove was cold; and the scrawny chickens and one disgruntled pig scattered away as they neared.

"The land of *sanook*," Kem murmured. "But there is little happiness here."

There was a little weaving loom in the house, where the woman had been weaving cloth. On one wall was a faded poster of Ho Chi Minh, next to a yellowed photograph of Mao.

"This is a Lao-type house," Durell said.

"Oh, yes," said Kem. "Over eight million Lao live in northeast Thailand. Ethnically, they are a branch of the Thai people, and they call themselves the 'Children of the Thai.' But many of them belong to the Pathet Lao, and lately, Peking organized a 'Free Thai' movement here to encourage terrorism

162

and insurrection against Bangkok. In 1965, the Chinese Foreign Minister, Chen Yi, called publicly for guerrilla warfare, and now the rebels are organized as the 'Thai Patriotic Front.' The gangsters of the Muc Tong work hand in glove with them."

They walked on.

Beyond some wild banana groves and tall bamboo that towered a hundred feet overhead, they abruptly found themselves entering a tribal village. There was no way to avoid it. The trail turned suddenly, and they were there. It was a typical fortified *wieng* in the Lao manner, following the course of another mountain stream. The houses were on stilts, with thatched roofs, teak verandas, a jumble of dogs, lean pigs, and chickens. Only women, children and old men were in sight. As Durell, ahead of Benjie and Kem, appeared, a silence fell over the people, who stopped what they were doing and stood and stared. One old man ran into his house and came out with a Sten gun, which he brandished at them and yelled something to his wife, who scuttled into the house, gathering up her children like a frightened, little brown hen.

The old man held the Sten gun as if he knew how to use it. Another man, his ribs showing through his open shirt, came out

163

with a Russian-made Kalashnikov rifle. Durell halted, and Benjie drew a long breath and stood frozen beside him.

"Speak to them, Flivver. Tell them we're friends."

The monk walked calmly toward the threatening guns. Except for a single barking dog that cowered in the shadows of a nearby house, the whole village had fallen dead silent. The sunlight gleamed on Kem's shaven head as he spoke quietly.

"We come as friend, old man. Where are your grown sons and daughters?"

The man with the Sten waved toward the valley. "They all work. All the young men and women. Who are you?"

"Travelers, pilgrims, seeking peace."

"Who is the bastard Chinese?"

"A good man, a kind man, a friend. May Buddha's gentle light fall upon you all."

"He looks strange to me. And the *fahrang* woman?"

"Another friend."

"What do they want here?"

"They look for the *fahrang* lady's brother. He was here. We come to find him."

"There are only Yunnan people, the engineers who build the road for certain others. Those Chinese are in the valley, too. They burned Xo Dong. Do you see it?" The old man pointed again. "We do not wish them to burn us, too."

From the village street, they could look down the valley to the river and a newly built road that started from a gorge about five miles away to the northeast. Tall granite cliffs and limestone scarps were capped with dense foliage that almost touched from each side over the pass. Durell used the binoculars to examine the scene. There were a number of trucks in the gorge, neatly hidden from possible air surveillance. There was some activity in the village on this side of the gorge, but the morning haze and the sharp black shadows of the mountainside made it difficult to see details.

More villagers had gathered, old men and women, and their faces were closed and hostile. A number of them were armed with a variety of guns. Durell turned back to the old man with the Sten, who seemed to be the leader.

Durell said, "We ask you again about the *fahrang* lady's brother."

"We know nothing. We say nothing. We wish to be left alone."

"Was he here?"

"We know nothing," the old man repeated. "It is I who ask questions. Your accent is terrible. I think you –"

165

Kem intervened smoothly. "It is of no consequence. We will journey on, old man."

"Father," said the man to the monk, "you must wait here for the authorities. They will be angry with us, if we let you go."

"And yet we must go," said Kem. "It is a holy mission, and we will continue with it."

Durell pointed down to the distant valley. "Do the Muc Tong frighten you?"

There was a murmur from the crowd of villagers. The old man swung his Sten gun nervously and shouted at them for silence. Fear built upon his anger, and he jabbed the gun at Durell and Benjie. Sweat gathered on the back of Durell's neck.

"You," said the old man to Durell. "Why do you ask about the Muc Tong? You are not one of them."

"You grow opium for them, do you not?"

"It is our business. We grow rice and tea and bananas, too. We grow for whoever pays us."

"And opium is profitable?"

The old man spoke in rage. "You look strange to me. Not Chinese, not *fahrang*. Why the holy monk walks with you is not my business. The *bhikkhu* may go. You must stay."

"We wish no trouble with you."

"You are a spy from Bangkok. I can see

that. All of you are spies. But we are believers in the Patriotic Front. The Front rules here. We pay them taxes, and they take our young men into their army. They take a reasonable share of our food. In return, they do not burn our *wieng*. We live in peace."

"It is the peace of slaves," Kem murmured.

"One moment." Benjie stepped forward, directly toward the threatening guns. "Phan Do, why do you not remember me? You were my foreman at the tea plantation. You worked for me for three years, you and your sons and your villagers."

"I do not know you," the old man snapped. "And my sons are soldiers now."

"They are opium smugglers," Benjie said. "Not an honorable profession. Phan, you are being foolish. Do not threaten us with your gun. We will go in peace."

"I cannot permit it."

"We will go," Kem said.

He walked ahead through the crowd, with Benjie, and Durell moved ahead through the villagers. For a moment, it looked as if they would close ranks against them, and there would be violence. Durell was aware of the old man pointing his Sten gun at their backs, but he did not look at Phan. Kem's saffron robe stood out brightly against the drab tribal costumes. The monk murmured to the women, touched a child's head in benediction. There was no fear in his eyes. One woman suddenly ran into her house and came out with a wooden bowl of rice, which she offered to the *bhikkhu*. Kem accepted it gravely. Another woman said, "It is a long time since we were permitted to have a *bhikku*. Stay with us, holy man!"

"I cannot. But I shall return," Kem said gently.

Phan shouted angrily at the other old man, but the women closed ranks and kept the armed men from interfering. Benjie's face was pale, but her green eyes were steady. Once, in the village street, she stumbled, and Durell caught her quickly.

"Keep walking."

"I want to look back. They'll shoot us."

"Don't. Stay near Flivver."

"What a hell of a name for a Buddhist monk," she said. "I don't know why I came up here with you."

There were posters of Mao-Tse-tung and a number of signs in Chinese calligraphy, and a propaganda flag calling for the death of all Western imperialists, plastered and painted on the village houses. Obviously, Bangkok's security forces made no effort to penetrate this stronghold of the insurgents.

168

The trail turned left, past a tall grove of bamboo, and went down toward the distant valley and the even more distant gorge. Durell heard the old man still shouting as they left the village behind them.

19

The village smelled of burned oil, cordite, dead bodies and offal. Xo Dong had died violently, the victim of a terrorist raid that had burned houses and fields and sent bullets smashing into women and children. Half the houses were razed, and provisions and river boats were stolen. Everything was stripped. Only a few rags moved forlornly from a rope of washing down by the river. It was nine o'clock in the morning.

A small tributary stream ran along the main village street and emptied into the wider river that came out of the gorge, three miles east along the border. This time, the absence of villagers was permanent. No one challenged them as they carefully entered the wrecked town. Not even a dog or a chicken had been left alive.

"Why did they do it?" Benjie murmured.

"Maybe because of Mike."

"I don't understand that."

"Maybe they gave Mike shelter and help," Durell said. "Don't think about it. It's a good place to make our headquarters."

"Here?" She was appalled at the desolation.

"Nobody will come back here for a long time. We'll be safe enough."

He discovered several houses that had escaped the raiders, near the river behind a screen of tall bamboo and banana trees. Durell chose one that seemed cleaner than the others, a wooden house with a wide veranda on poles built over the water. Most of the primitive furniture still remained, and a ruined motorcycle testified to a certain amount of affluence for the family that had lived here. It had been a long hike over the mountain from the tea plantation where they had hidden the plane, but if the sound of the Apache's engines had made any alarm among the smugglers farther up the valley, there was no hint of it. Durell saw that Benjie's face was too tight and too pale, and he distracted her by suggesting the use of the charcoal stove to make them a decent breakfast during the respite.

"Yes, there's some rice. Even some bacon."

"Leave the bacon. It'll probably be spoiled. Rice and tea will be fine," Durell said.

"I'm not hungry, though."

"I am. Go on, Benjie."

"How do you plan to locate Mike?" She stood on the veranda of the abandoned house and squinted east into the morning sun that glittered on the muddy river. "Mike could be anywhere in these hills. Anywhere. There are a hundred trails going in every direction. Nobody pays attention to the borders here. Savag's troops are supposed to maintain checkpoints in this district, but I haven't seen anything of them."

"I'm sure they're around," Durell said.

"But what about Mike?"

Kem said quietly, "I will find him. You two can stay here. I will be back by noon, I promise. It will be safe enough for me. The villagers will help me – especially the women." The *bhikkhu* grinned. "If Mike is alive, I will learn where he is."

"He must be dead," Benjie said, discouraged. "The whole valley is swarming with Muc Tong and Red forces."

"If he is dead, then it is important to learn that, too," Kem said gravely.

He left his pack in the house and made Benjie a *wai*, palms pressed together

171

serenely. Durell watched him for a minute or two as he lifted his orange robe and waded across the shallow stream that emptied into the river nearby. The bright robe flickered against the green of the jungle. There was another sign nailed to a teak tree on the other side of the river, which also read *'Ham'* – forbidden. A board under it was scrawled in Thai script, announcing the territory as belonging to the People's Liberation Army of the United Thai Front. They always used attractive names and slogans, Durell thought grimly, and they always meant the opposite of what they said.

He did not like the waiting. Patience was a prime necessity in his business, and waiting and watching and learning was part of the game, and sometimes to keep alive simply by sitting still and out-guessing the enemy in silence. But he didn't like it. He was not happy that Flivver had gone out alone, while he remained here with Benjie, but it made sense to let the monk do the scouting.

Benjie made the tea and rice and they ate together in the shade of the veranda, under the overhanging thatch roof. A hot wind blew off the river and kept the smells of the destroyed town from touching them. The girl was distant, thinking thoughts that Durell could not guess.

172

"You look tired," he said quietly.

"I am. I don't often admit it. But it's not just from last night and today and all the things about Mike. It's just all the years in the past."

"Are you worried about your losses at the logging camp?"

She shook her head. In the shadows, the planes of her face were softened. She had tied back her long hair with a stray piece of bright green ribbon that made her eyes look more emerald than before. There was a rip in her shirt that exposed one sun-browned shoulder. Her lower lip was full. Her mouth drooped.

"All these years," she went on. "What for? What's it gotten me? I thought I had to take care of Mike, my little brother, and play the mother role to him. But he's a big boy now, and I ought to accept it, Sam. I'm not his keeper any more."

"He doesn't want you to be his keeper."

"I suppose not. I suppose he's always resented the way I've tried to boss him around." She smiled ruefully. "It's not been easy, playing mother and father to him all these years."

"And you never paid much attention to yourself."

"I'm afraid I haven't. I'm a mess, I guess.

173

Not the sort of girl you'd take to a New York cocktail party, eh?" She laughed a little. "It isn't that I don't like myself the way I am. But I wonder if it's all been worth it – the fighting for business advantages, keeping accounts, looking for new opportunities, competing with men in their world – well, I'm suddenly tired of it. I'd like to stay right here, forever, where no one would ever find us."

"We can stay only until Flivver comes back."

She said, "Do you trust him?"

"I have to."

"But you don't trust me?"

"I think I do."

"But you're not sure," she persisted.

"No."

She said, "You make me feel dirty, with all your suspicions. I feel as if I need a bath."

He smiled. "We both do. And there's the river."

She was startled. "Now?"

"Why not? It's the last peaceful moment we'll have for a while," Durell said. "We ought to enjoy it."

"Are you making a pass at me, Sam?"

"Yes."

She made a low whistling sound, laughing

uncertainly, and said, "Wow. It's been a long time."

"Too long, I think," Durell said quietly. He took her hand. "Come on."

Her pale body moved smoothly in the clear water of the mountain brook that tumbled down above the ruined village of Xo Dong. Sunlight dappled the quick-moving surface of the stream, and tall bamboo and wild flowers brightened the rocky banks. There was only the sound of the rushing water and the occasional murmur of the mountain wind, accented by the clear notes of brightly colored birds that flitted in the trees. Durell watched the girl swimming naked and alone in the brook. Her long hair streamed wetly behind her. She lifted a sun-browned arm that formed an abrupt white line above her breasts. He was surprised by the richness of her slender body.

"Come on in, Sam. The water's fine."

He left his clothes and gun on the bank, within quick reach if necessary. The dynamite and Benjie's haversack were in the abandoned native house, only fifty yards away.

"Sam..."

She swam toward him, her hands reaching. They felt cold, colder than the water.

175

Her green eyes were brilliant. Her smile was uncertain, and he thought he saw fear in her.

"It's such an awful thing," she whispered, as their bodies touched.

"What is?"

"With all this destruction around us – all the tragedies of these poor people – for you and me to spend the hour doing – doing –"

"Making love?" he asked.

"Yes."

"Do you want to?"

"If you do."

"Why? There must have been some men."

"No."

"You turned them down?"

"I – I was too busy. There was no – no –"

"Profit in it?"

She pulled angrily away. "Oh, you are cruel!"

He swam after her. The bright birds flickered in the foliage that overhung the pool. There were no other sounds. The sunlight made soft shadows under the bamboo trees on the bank.

"Don't think about it," he said.

"I can't help it. I'm confused, Sam. I – I don't know what I am, any more."

"You're a woman," he told her. "And a beautiful woman, at that."

20

Afterward, she sat by herself, naked in the sun, and combed her long hair, watching her reflection in the brook. She still smiled, but there were no secrets in her face now. She looked open and drowsy, and as she bent over the water, intent on her hair, Durell retrieved his gun and looked toward the deserted broken village.

"Get dressed."

"Why?" she asked. "There's plenty of time."

"Kem is coming back."

"I don't hear him."

"He's coming. Get dressed."

She splashed toward him, her hips heavy with the effort of wading through the water. She was changed. Durell kept watching the village street, his gun in his hand.

"What is it, Sam?"

"It's all right."

"Are you angry with me?"

"Why should I be?"

"I wasn't very good, was I?"

"You were wonderful," he said. "Please
177

get dressed, Benjie. Kem is a devout Buddhist, a monk, and he shouldn't see you like this."

"What could he see?"

He smiled. "It's in your eyes."

She went toward the bungalow they were using. He thought he heard her singing. A moment later, the saffron robe of the monk appeared at the end of the ruined street.

Kem sat down in the dust, his feet tucked under his thighs, his hands resting palms upward in his lap. His slanted eyes regarded Durell gravely. Without eyebrows, his thoughts were difficult to perceive. There was sweat on his shaven scalp, and his robe was stained with dust. Durell sat down facing him. "Did you find him, Flivver?"

"Yes, I found Mike."

"Alive?"

"He is alive. I did not see him. I only learned where he is hiding. But he is hurt. A small thing, only a turned ankle, but he cannot walk very well. He is alone, in the hills over there." Kem did not use his hands to gesture. He simply looked beyond Durell, down the valley toward the distant, hazy gorge. "It is a very big caravan, Sam."

"The dope smugglers?"

"There are two hundred, maybe three hundred men. They have gathered all the

178

crop, and even some of the stuff that has
been refined in village factories. There are
jeeps, trucks, mules and horses. Some of it
will be rafted downstream toward the Ping
River. They are very open about their work."

"When will they leave?"

"Tomorrow morning."

"Then we're on time to stop them,"
Durell said.

"Against three hundred men? Not very
possible."

Benjie came out of the bungalow, dressed
in her denims, boots and man's shirt. Her
hair was brushed out and tied back with
another bit of ribbon. She walked lightly,
smiling.

Kem said, "So the lady boss is a woman,
after all."

"Yes. I told her you were perceptive."

"I remember my school days in the States.
They were good times. But I do not regret
devoting my life to Buddha."

"First, pay your debt to us," Durell said.
"Are you sure Mike wasn't in contact with
the Muc Tong?"

"I was told he was alone." Kem turned his
shaven head and studied the ruins of the
village. "The people of Xo Dong fled into
the hills. Some of them helped Mike. Others
are working practically as slaves for the Muc

Tong. Those who helped Mike did so out of loyalty, from when they worked on the tea plantation. They may be with him on the mountain."

Benjie joined them, and Durell told her about Mike and the smuggling caravan, and turned back to the monk. "Are the Muc Tong well armed?"

"They get paid in arms, they use the black market in weapons in Bangkok, Saigon, Vientiane – everywhere – and pay the insurgents with part of their weapons, too. Only the caravan masters and the bosses get paid in gold. The others are merely mercenaries."

"And the Thai Third Army?"

"They never come here. They are supposed to check the border, but they never do so in this area. However, some of the villagers have seen General Uva Savag. They hate him. He has been cruel to the mountain people, and because of this, they almost prefer the Muc Tong and the Communist rebels."

"How do we get to Mike?" Benjie interrupted.

Kem stood up. "We must walk."

The trail led downriver for a mile, then crossed the stream on a sandy ford. The valley bottom was now hot and breathless,

180

although a few puffy clouds had appeared to the south. Durell held them back until he had scanned as much of both banks of the muddy river as he could see. The foliage was dense, green, impenetrable. Nothing moved on the ground. Birds flashed in the trees, and once he thought he saw a monkey. There was no sound except the splashing of the river.

"Let's go," Benjie said impatiently.

"Wait."

"But Mike needs help."

"Keep your voice down. When you cross the ford, move fast. Don't look back. Get on the other side and sit down. You and Kem go first, I'll cover you. I think we're being watched."

Benjie looked at the silent forests around them, squinted at the sun, wiped sweat from her forehead, then waded into the water. Kem tucked his robe up between his legs and followed. Durell stood in the shadows of the bamboo trees, his gun in hand.

He was finished with Kem. He did not need the monk any more. The best course would be to send him back to Bangkok, to go under cover again, before something exposed him as a sleeper agent. He might be useful again, in the future. K Section would be pleased, if he did this. But he did not

181

think Kem would quit now. Kem was enjoying himself.

Benjie and the monk reached the other side. He looked at them, half hidden under the foliage, and then waded out into the river himself. The sky, the forests, the mountains watched him. He moved quickly, but the bottom was soft underfoot, and he carried the weight of the dynamite on his back.

The rifle shot made a thin crack, like the breaking of a tree branch.

Water spurted and wet his right knee and thigh. A little higher, Durell thought, and the slug would have gone through the explosives on his back.

He heard Benjie call out and surged forward, halfway across the river. He slid sidewise, favoring his left knee, which gave him twinges even now as he fought the river current. The rifle popped again. The bullet made a hot wind past his cheek. A marksman. Not too far away. Upriver, toward the gorge, which was not visible here because of a bend in the stream. Benjie called out again. Durell felt the bottom give way under his feet, his left knee twinged again, and he went down up to his hips in the water. The third bullet whined over his head.

He reached the opposite bank. Kem

reached out a strong hand and pulled him up. The monk's green eyes were grave.

"Who was it? Did you see?"

"Stay here."

"He has a rifle. Your gun is too small, too –"

"Stay here. Watch Benjie."

He left them, moving fast upstream toward the area where he thought he had spotted the glint off the rifle. He couldn't see it from here now, but he had the place marked in his mind. He tried to think what the man would do. Retreat, maybe. Or stalk him, confident of his superior weapon. Durell slipped the dynamite pack from his shoulders and paused in leafy shadows above the river bank. He heard the soft sound of a boot on the forest floor. A bird squawked, made a flash of orange and red overhead. Shadows moved with the movement of the wind. Durell halted in the shadow of a tree trunk.

The man came carefully, lifting each foot with exaggerated caution, his Russian-made AK-47 held in both hands. He wore a Thai Army uniform, with a forage cap carrying the emblem of the Third Security Force. His eyes shifted, searching the glittery surface of the river through the foliage. When he was one step past Durell, he halted, sensing another presence, suddenly aware of danger.

He was too late.

Durell hit the back of his neck with the edge of his left hand, used his right foot for a blow to the kidneys, and as the breath went out of the man with a rush, Durell caught at the swinging gun, closed his right hand on the barrel, pulled it free, then swung the stock into the other's frightened face. Blood smashed from the round nose, obscured the white, staring eyes. The man fell back, seated, his hands behind him breaking the fall. The eyes glazed. Durell hit him again, not sparing anything, and the body rolled down the slope, breaking a few shrubs before it sprawled in the mud of the river bank.

Durell did not think there had been too much noise.

He straightened, breathed lightly, and put away his own gun and took up the welcome weight of the AK-47. He did not know if the man was dead or not. He did not think there were any others nearby. This one had just happened to wander down the river, maybe looking for a refugee woman, maybe hoping for something to steal.

He turned away, and went to Benjie and Kem.

"Here, take the rifle," he told Kem.

"No, thank you."

"I ought to send you home, you know."

"But I will not go. Did you think I would go now?"

Benjie said, "Are you all right, Sam? I'll take the gun. I don't have Flivver's religious compunctions."

"You Westerners are all bloodthirsty," Kem said.

"So were Savag's Mongol ancestors," Durell replied. He added, "I think it was one of Savag's men. Unless he was a Muc Tong, wearing a stolen uniform." He picked up the dynamite pack and adjusted it on his shoulders again. "Let's go on."

21

The place was like an animal burrow, a broken-down peasant's hut halfway up the limestone scarp to the top of the valley's rim, a half mile from the village at the mouth of the pass where the caravan was gathered. The roof of the hut had fallen down at one end, making a triangular shelter that held a pallet of reeds, a small charcoal stove, a worn knapsack, a field transmitter, and several empty bottles of whiskey. Two tribesmen from Xo Dong, sturdy men with bandy legs and green headbands around their coarse black hair, led the way. They carried no weapons. The camp site was deep in the woods, but not far from a terraced slope where opium poppies had recently been grown.

"Benjie. Hi, Sam. You took your time getting here. Almost too late. Didn't you get the May Day?" Mike said.

"We did the best we could," Durell said.

"Did you bring the blasting stuff?"

"It's here."

"My damned ankle. Stupid thing. You try to reckon every possibility, but you can't foresee a pebble in your way."

Benjie stared at her brother as if unable to believe it. Mike was filthy, his hair looked as if it hadn't been combed for days, and his clothes were torn and ragged. He had lost or thrown away one of his boots, and his right ankle was crudely bandaged in dirty rags. He used a stick to climb to his feet and shake hands with Durell. He did not offer any further greeting to his sister, and Durell sensed an immediate hostility between them. But somehow the irrespressible nature of the man came through in his broad, freckled

186

face, his tight grin, his quick manner of speech. Mike Slocum looked at Kem.

"Who's the *bhikkhu*?"

"A guide," Durells aid.

"We don't need him. Too many moral compunctions. You can't tell which way the Sangha may jump, these days. Against the government today, against the rebels tomorrow. Send him away."

"Flivver is an old friend. He went to Williams College. Your old alma mater."

"Hell. No kidding?" Mike grinned again. "Me, I flunked out. Benjie really burned my ass, that time. Always yelling when I got into a little trouble. We've got trouble here, too."

"Much worse than you think," Benjie said tightly.

"How is that?"

She swung an arm toward the valley and the distant Muc Tong caravan. "Durell thinks you've been having fun and games, for a profit, with those people down there."

"That's a laugh."

"Is it true, Mike?" she asked.

"Listen, Benjie, don't ride me now. I was having some sport up here, until you came along."

"You look it. Always playing games, always leaving the dirty work to me, making me pick up after you." She drew a deep

187

breath. "All right, I don't want any part of it. Not any more. Not you, not Sam. Just ignore me."

"That will be a pleasure," Mike snapped. His eyes gleamed with old angers, then he looked at Kem and said, "Williams, huh?"

"True."

"But you're really a *bhikkhu* now?"

"My life is dedicated to the good work of the Sangha."

"You look like a son of a bitch, to me. But never mind, as long as you helped Sam bring the dynamite here."

Durell said, "You didn't answer Benjie, Mike."

"About the Muc Tong? Me and them?"

"You and them, yes."

"Shit," Mike Slocum said.

"They never approached you to use Thai Star transport facilities for their opium smuggling?"

"What are you talking about? Of course they did. A couple of times. Even tried to use the old badger game on me, when I had a cute trick upstairs over the Arrow Cafe. Blackmail, threats, attempts at extortion. A certain Mr. Chuk was the heavy. Know him?"

"We've met."

"But nothing. Why are you here, if you

think I'm in cahoots with those creeps down there?"

"Just playing the odds," Durell said.

"Yeah. Well. You sent me in here, Cajun. True, I asked for the job. Thought it would be fun. It would be, too, if I hadn't cracked the stupid ankle. Got a lot of data for you, and for that creep, James D. James. How do you ever pick Controls like that character?"

"Washington does it," Durell said.

"Well, I think he's in it, up to his sweet neck. You and me, we're the fall guys for him. He never wants us to come home, you can count on it. The trouble is, it's that Miss Ku that he keeps around, the little bitch. She's General Uva Savag's girl, did you know that?"

"I thought she might be."

"And Savag is getting paid off to leave the caravans alone in this security area. What the hell, everybody's out to snatch a piece of the action."

"Not you?" Durell asked.

"You bastard." Mike lunged forward, swinging his stick at Durell's head. He was a stocky, powerful man, with massive shoulders and a tough, muscular torso. His bloodshot eyes were suddenly filled with murderous rage. The blow could have been fatal. But Durell easily sidestepped, hearing

189

a murmur from the village refugees who watched in confusion. As the stick whistled downward, Durell caught it and Mike's ankle gave way. He grunted with pain, fell on his hands and knees, cursing angrily, and crawled to one side of the hut.

Benjie said contemptuously, "Mike, you're a fool."

His face shone with sweat. "What's with you? You look different. Did Cajun get to you?"

"Shut up. You're lucky if he doesn't kill you."

"Why should he? We're on the same team."

"He's not too sure of that."

"Ah." Mike made a sound of disgust, looked up at Durell, and with his mercural change of temperament, grinned engagingly. "You're not sore at me, are you, Cajun?"

"No."

"You bring anything to drink?"

"A little Mekong."

"Great."

Durell got the bottle of whiskey from the haversack and handed it to the seated man. The villagers looked disappointed. The wind that blew up from the valley felt hot and dry, but there were more clouds in the sky to the south, and Durell heard a distant rumble of

190

thunder. It was too early for the monsoons, unless the rains came exceptionally soon. Probably a mango shower in the hills, he thought. He hoped it wouldn't interfere with what he had in mind. He watched Mike gulp the liquor. Mekong was powerful stuff. Mike drank it as if it were water.

"That's enough," Durell said.

"You bet. Friends?"

"We'll see. Tell me what you've been up to, here."

Mike belched and put his weight on his elbows and shoulders as he leaned back. He smelled as if he hadn't bathed in a week, which he probably hadn't, and there were deep lines of exhaustion on his normally cheerful face. He pushed his hair away from her eyes.

"Yeah. You want to be briefed. You sent me in to check out the insurgent movement in this area." Mike laughed. "Then Jimmy James gave me the real job, under the first cover apparatus. The Muc Tong, no less. The drug smugglers and the refineries they've established in all these little villages. None of these people love Bangkok, you know. They're easily subverted. Especially when Bangkok sends a sadistic bastard like General Savag to run things up here. So the people cooperate with the caravans, sell them

191

the poppies, set up home manufacturies to do the refining. It's bigger than you can imagine. And tightly organized. What you see down there is the main caravan for this season. Usually they send the stuff down the Mekong River to Saigon or Vientiane, or down the Ping to Bangkok in smaller lots. But it's been a bumper year, a great crop. And until they paid off Savag, he kept bothering them. Now they've got the green light, and there must be twenty million dollars' worth of the stuff, at Western prices, down there on those donkeys and trucks. But there are also three hundred armed hoodlums, too, Sam. So I was stymied."

"Tell me about Savag. Was he in the area?"

Mike shifted his ankle painfully. "The villagers say they see him now and then, down there with the Muc Tong."

"And a Major Luk?"

"Never heard of him. But the locals are sure of Savag. They're not apt to forget the man who burns their houses, kills their men, and rapes the wives, huh?"

Durell nodded and got up and walked out of the hut and crossed to a ledge of granite that overlooked the river valley. They were less than a mile from the caravan camp, but several thousand feet above in elevation. The road was a dusty ribbon that began at the narrow pass with its vine-covered cliffs and dark holes of caves. He used the binoculars to study what was going on down there. Behind him, Kem talked quietly to the tribesmen, and Benjie's voice was harsh and uncompromising as she spoke to her brother.

There were twenty-two jeeps and eighteen trucks and one armored vehicle. Each jeep carried .50-caliber machineguns. The men were not uniformed, but they looked hardened and tough, living in tents and some of the riverside houses. Durell searched through the glasses for what might be the headquarters. He counted over fifty donkeys, then gave up. The men were hard at work in the noon heat, loading the vehicles. He turned the binoculars back to the riverside houses. Banners were strung between some of the houses, and he could make out Chinese calligraphy, white on red, and a portrait of Mao and an unfamiliar Chinese face. A little apart from the caravaneers were some tents that had a military formation to them, and by watching steadily, he finally defined a bunker set deep in a grove of bamboo at one end of the village. He kept the glasses fixed steadily on that spot.

"Sam?"

It was Benjie. He didn't turn to look at her.

"Sam, Mike wants to explain what he wants to do with the dynamite."

"I know what he wants to do with it."

Two uniformed men came out of the bunker, carrying automatic rifles slung over their shoulders. They were the first uniforms Durell had spotted, and even from this distance, he could see they were Third Army outfits, similar to the one worn by the rifleman at the river ford. He kept watching.

"Sam? I'm worried about Mike," Benjie said.

"It's all right."

"Do you believe him?"

"Yes, I do."

"Well, I don't," she said tightly. "I don't trust him. Even as a kid, he was up to some sly scheme of his own, all the time. He has a lot of money with him."

"Money?"

"Burmese, Thai bahts, American dollars."

"How much?"

"Over thirty thousand, I think."

James D. James would not have provided Mike Slocum with anything near that sum. Durell lowered the glasses and looked at Benjie. Her face was sober and strained, questioning him. From somewhere in the

194

little camp, he heard Kem ringing his little silver bell. He hoped the sound would not carry too far over the wooded mountainside, but he didn't think he ought to stop the monk from going about his religious rites.

"Where do you think Mike got it?" Durell asked.

"I don't know. Maybe he stole it from me, from our joint bank accounts in Bangkok."

"Wishful thinking. You owed Chuk's bank on your notes. Did you have that much?"

"No."

"Then where did he get it?"

"He won't say. I don't think you should ask him, either."

Durell watched the bunker down below. A third uniformed man came out of the hole in the ground. This one was clad in the black pajama outfit of the Pathet Lao, and he carried a revolver in his belt. Officer type. The face was just a face. The three uniformed men went over to the trucks and jeeps and donkeys, and were lost in the crowd. Durell looked at his watch. The wind had died and the sun was merciless, although thunder still rolled beyond the soft, wooded mountains. It was one o'clock. He looked flatly at Benjie.

"Let's eat," he said.

22

"They'll head west and south, at dawn.
To do that, they have to go through this
gorge, and then past the tea platation. I
know this place, Cajun." Mike laughed. "I
once had a geologist friend who stayed with
us, when the tea farm was still working.
He said this whole scarp of schist and
limestone is rotten, honeycombed with caves
and faults. A few years ago there was a
government team from Bangkok nosing
around here, to consider building a dam that
would block the pass and build up an
artificial lake for irrigation. Nothing came
of it, though. So that's why I asked for the
dynamite.

"To blow the cliff down?"

"Right. Just when the caravan passes
through at dawn tomorrow. The charges
would have to be placed and timed pretty
carefully, though."

Mike was panting from the grueling climb
to the top of the cliff. They had been guided
by Missa tribesmen out of Xo Dong, and
Mike labored slowly with the aid of his

wooden stick. He had a Chinese automatic rifle slung over his shoulder.

"What do you think?" he asked.

"We can do it," Durell said, "if we can stay hidden through the night."

"Lots of caves here. We'll just sweat it out."

Durell walked over to Benjie. She sat on the ledge, her knees drawn up under her chin, and stared passively across the gorge. Her eyes were remote. He sat down beside her.

"Did you ask him about the money?" she said.

"Not yet."

"What are you waiting for? To really nail him to the cross?"

"I need him, right now. Later, we'll see."

"How can you be so cold about it? He's my brother, after all. I feel sick about it. I shouldn't have told you. Especially after you and I ..."

"I'd have found out, anyway," he said.

"I feel like a Judus," she whispered. "If Mike stole the money from me, or accepted it from the Muc Tong, I guess it doesn't make any difference. I want to help him, Sam. What can I do? Since you and I – in the river ..."

Her voice trailed off. She didn't look at

him. Durell got up and stood beside her. "I haven't seen the evidence yet," he said. "But it could have been planted. Maybe you put it there, yourself, in the first moments when we found him."

Her body tightened, and her shoulders hunched as if she had a chill. "Go away," she whispered.

"Did you?"

"Please!"

He walked away from her.

Durell spent two hours climbing up and down the face of the cliff, careful to avoid walking in a line tangent to the sight of the caravan men below. There were trails going up and down, and they had been used until recently, and perhaps were still being used by the local tribesmen. The caravan people moved about with open freedom, as if sure of their security. Their only guards were within several hundred yards of the edge of the camp. Durell moved in quite close, to watch their routine. Most of the loading was finished. The men ate an early meal, cooking over open fires, unconcerned. The pickets were back for their supper and sometimes were not replaced, leaving gaps in the defense perimeter. Durell hoped for a glimpse of more officers coming out of the bunker. Several black-uniformed Pathet Lao

198

and two men in Thai uniforms came and went around the bunker. Perhaps the Thai outfits were stolen, to be used if the caravan were stopped on the way toward Bangkok. The organization seemed to be loose and easy, not really military. Gangsters and smugglers were not given to too much discipline. When the shadows deepened in the mountain pass, and the last sunlight was lost behind heavy, gathering clouds, he made his way back up the cliff.

He was halfway up when they caught him.

The trail at this point was narrow, twisting around a bulge in the sheer face of the rock cliff of crumbling limestone. They were waiting in silence around the bend, not moving, their weapons ready. It was not that he had been noisy or careless. They must have spotted him when he was down below, starting the ascent to rejoin Mike and Benjie. They carried rifles, and the black muzzles were steady and hard, like their eyes. Three of them. And an officer. Uniforms like those worn among the caravaneers, but legitimate. Thai security patrol.

"Please do not move, Mr. Durell. My men are well trained. These are my best."

Durell did not move. "Major Luk?"

"I am honored that you remember me."

"I owe you some thanks for letting Miss Slocum and me out of Savag's barracks."

"The General was very angry."

"And he put you out here in the boondocks?"

"My duties bring me here."

"With just three men?"

"The patrol is on my own initiative."

Durell remembered the Thai officer's pride in his nation, his uncertainty about Uva Savag, and his professionalism. Major Luk's face was bland and smooth, untroubled by the sultry heat of evening. Thunder crashed suddenly, much louder and nearer. The day was dying. Only a few pale streaks of sunlight still glowed over the hills.

"Please," said Luk. "You will not resist. I must have your word."

"Am I under arrest?"

"Not precisely. As I said, the patrol is my own. I know who and what you are, Mr. Durell, and I am not surprised to find you here. I have scouted your party up on the cliff."

"You have bigger fish to fry." Durell waved to the glowing caravan fires in the valley. "Those people don't seem to be worried about your border security force."

"There has been no action ordered against them."

200

"Because Savag gets paid off?"

"Yes, I think so."

"Put your guns away. I believe we're friends."

"Possibly." Luk smiled. "I have my duty to do. My men do not understand English. They follow and obey my orders. Each has been a victim of Savag's temper – they each have lost rank and privilege for minor infractions. That is, they did their duty as they are supposed to, which annoyed our General, who has another view of what should be done here." The major smiled again. His black eyes were opaque in the growing dusk. He spoke quietly to the three men, who lowered their guns reluctantly.

Durell could have taken them at that moment. It was all a matter of attitude, of movement and response. The odds were not bad. Two of the men had their guns pointed downward. The third cradled his weapon in his arm, pointed out over the gorge. Only Major Luk kept his hand on his holstered revolver.

It was the certainty of noisy alarm that checked Durell. He could have used his own gun before the others moved, lulled as they were by Luk's command. But he didn't think Luk would go down easily. And if there was shooting, the caravan would be alerted. Not worth it, Durell decided.

"Well, then, here we are," Major Luk said. "The tribesmen say your friends have dynamite. I can understand your plans. You must permit me to join you."

"Savag will nail your hide to a tree," Durell said.

"I do only what I think must be done."

On any mission, the pattern shifts constantly. New elements enter, old ones vanish. Major Luk might or might not be sincere. Each new danger had to be weighed and balanced. Luk might be a spy for Savag; he might be working with the Muc Tong. But there seemed to be little choice, at the moment.

"All right," Durell said. "Come along."

Kem had found some Buddhist monks, hermits who lived in nearby caves, and they had joined the little party. With darkness, they chose one of the nearest caverns, and all of them tried to make themselves comfortable. For two hours in the dim starlight, Durell continued to explore the cliff over the gorge, looking for a site for the dynamite, but found nothing that would guarantee a devastating rock slide onto the road below. They ate cold rice for supper.

Thunder rolled overhead and turned the night totally black, forcing Durell to abandon the dangerous climb around the cliff. When the rain came, its force was enormous, hammering at the mountains as if it would never end. Major Luk and his three men sat apart from the others in the cave. The Missa tribesmen were angry at the presence of the soldiers, but no one left the shelter during the height of the shower.

"I am a demolition expert myself," Major Luk said quietly to Durell. "When the rain ends, the moon should be out, and we can place the charges then."

"Before dawn," Mike insisted. "They move out then."

"Agreed."

The cave's opening was screened by black water that fell heavily down the face of the cliff. It seemed never to end. Thunder rolled and shook the earth and drowned out the subdued chanting of Kem and his newly found hermit monks. There were eight of them, with shaved scalps and dirty robes. Incense curled from an ornate bowl one of them carried. Kem continued in deep conversation with them during their ceremonies. None of the pilgrim monks spoke to the tribesmen or Durell.

"Will they help us, if we need them?" he asked Kem.

The monk shrugged. "These men are very holy. They have come here and lived here for eight years. Each year, they have permitted another pilgrim to join them in meditation."

"What do they meditate about?"

"The evils and the end of the world."

Durell pointed to the black mouth of the cave, "There's evil right outside, down in the valley. Have you told them about it?"

"I have explained why we are here. They are considering it. But they will not speak to strangers. They speak only to me because we are all members of the Sangha. It is doubtful if they will act." Kem's eyes glowed. "They are indeed the holiest of men, Sam. The eighth year is almost ended, and soon they will choose another to join them for the ninth. They say the cycle must not be broken."

Durell considered the circle of tattered old men. Some had small prayer wheels, others simply sat with eyes closed in contemplation. "They won't interfere with us, Flivver?"

"They have renounced the wicked world, and seek only to achieve merit for their next lives."

The rain fell. Nothing could be seen in the black night, except when jagged lightning

204

flashed and the mountains shook with the thunderclaps. In the intermittent blue light, Durell tried to see what was happening where the caravan was camped. He looked at his watch and was surprised to find it was almost midnight. Unless the rain stopped soon, there would be no chance to go out on the cliff and find a proper place for the dynamite.

He went to Mike, who sat in one of the deeper recesses of the cave, around a jut of rock that made it safe to light a clay oil lamp in which the wick sputtered and gave off a rancid, smoky smell. Benjie sat with him, talking quietly, when he approached. She looked up and got to her feet.

"Sam . . ."

"We'll talk now."

"I don't want to hear it, Sam. Mike is lying."

"To hell with you both," Mike said.

Benjie walked away, her shoulders stiff, as if she expected a blow in the back. Durell sat down. There was a half-empty bottle of Mekong in Mike's lap, and he offered it vaguely, his face shadowed by the guttering lamp. Durell shook his head and Mike grunted and shifted his weight back against the wall to favor his bandaged ankle.

"Benjie says you know about the money."

"That's right."

"I just counted it," Mike said. "A neat little package. It comes to about thirty-two thousand U.S. dollars. A guy would have a real ball with all that."

"Where did you get it, Mike?"

The other's eyes were muddy with liquor. He smelled of sweat and pain. "I found it, old buddy. Are you going to make something out of it?"

"Where did you find it?"

"In Xo Dong. Actually, I didn't even know I had it. Old Gujiwandara Phan must have slipped it into my pack. I was so uptight about my ankle I never realized it, until Benjie snooped around first thing, always playing Mama and Big Sister. She's a bitch, even if she is my only family."

"You didn't know it was in your pack?"

"No, I didn't know."

"But you think it came from this Gujiwandara?"

"He was the headman of Xo Dong."

"Where would a tribesman get that kind of money?"

Mike shrugged. He looked angry and defensive. "How would I know? I think he'd collected it over the year from his villagers, to pay off the Muc Tong. But then he didn't

206

pay them off, did he? Because they burned the place down."

"Where is this headman now?"

"He's dead."

"That's convenient."

"If you don't believe me, to hell with you."

"Could someone else have planted the money on you?"

"Oh sure," Mike said, "Benjie could have done it."

"Why would she do that?"

"Come to think of it, maybe she really did."

"Why?" Durell asked again.

"Listen, Cajun, don't grill me. I know you think it's important, but I took on this job for you, I'm just a hired hand, in it for the kicks and salary, and nothing else. I'm not in the drug racket. I never was. God knows, I can't keep any money in my pocket, and my sister always complains. I've got no head for business, either, and Benjie really runs everything connected with Thai Star. Just the same, old buddy, I'm not about to sell out to a bunch of bastards like the Muc Tong. Now, you'd better believe it, or we part ways, here and now."

Durell said, "Maybe Benjie smothered you with too much care and affection, Mike, but you've made a grave charge against her, saying she might have planted the bribe money on you."

"Hell, I only say she *might* have done it. She's been up a tree lately, being squeezed by Chuk, back in Bangkok. He holds all the Thai Star notes. He gave us a lot of labor trouble, too, ran up our costs with delays and strikes and squeeze money. The Thai Star is Benjie's whole life, and she'd do anything to save it."

"Even to being a traitor?"

"She wouldn't look at it that way."

"Why would she want to make *you* look suspicious?"

Mike said, "To cover herself. She's afraid of you."

Durell suddenly remembered the girl as she had been in the pool. He shook his head. "But you can't remember where the money came from, or how it got in your pack?"

"Listen," Mike said, "would I be working here to knock off the caravan with a landslide, if I'd taken their cash to lay off? It doesn't make sense."

"It could make sense, if you radiophoned me to get me up here into the hands of the Muc Tong," Durell said.

Mike stared. "Oh, brother." His voice hardened with anger. "You want the pack?

You want the money?" He shifted about, dug furiously into his battered canvas kit, and dumped the contents, soap, razor, a few cans of food, a Colt .45, some cartridge clips, an empty wallet, two pens and a compass on the dirt floor of the cave.

"Jesus," he said. "It's gone."

Durell said nothing.

Mike looked at him. "Benjie must have taken it."

Durell got up and walked through the cave toward the entrance, circling the monks who still chanted softly in a tight little group nearby. The men from Xo Dong sat apart near the cave mouth, watching the black rain pour down. They looked at him curiously. Kem came in off the ledge outside. His robe was sopping wet, clinging to his lean frame. His bald head gleamed with rain water.

"She is out there somewhere, Sam."

"Benjie?"

"She walked out into the rain, out on the trail. I just happened to look up and saw her go. So I went after her. But it's too black, too dangerous in the rain. I couldn't see her. I called to her, but she didn't answer."

Durell said, "Are you sure it was Benjie?"

"I haven't forgotten what a woman looks like," the *bhikkhu* said.

"Was she carrying anything?"

209

"Her haversack, yes." The monk looked worried. "Perhaps she will soon come back."

But Benjie didn't come back. She was gone.

23

The rain ended at two in the morning. Thunder rolled away to the north, and lightning still flashed there, but a warm wind cleared the night sky and presently there was the welcome glow of the moon rising over the deep chasm. Its light showed the road below, under the heavy overhang of the cliff. From outside the cave, Durrell could still see a few lights in the caravan camp. A truck motor was started up and revved, as someone tested the engine. The distant sound soon died away.

There was no sign of Benjie. The trail led to the top of the cliff, and he followed it with Kem, and presently they came to bamboo thickets and trees and the trail forked both east and west. There was no way to tell which way Benjie had taken. Major Luk appeared at his heels, with one of his men.

"I have sent my other troopers to look in

the valley for Miss Slocum," the Thai said. "Possibly she went out for privacy, and sheltered from the storm in another cave."

Durell was carrying the dynamite, wires and detonator. He looked at the sky and estimated they had about three hours before dawn. Some time before that, the caravan would start up and head east, through the pass. Give it two hours, he thought. Allow for error. He turned back to the cliff.

"My man is a demolition expert," Luk said tentatively.

"So am I," Durell told him.

They worked their way below the cave, clinging to wet and precarious handholds on the cliff. The dynamite pack dragged heavily on Durell's back. There were no tracks below the cave, and they had to pick and choose each grip with care, in the uncertain light of the moon. At the same time, they were visible from the caravan camp, half a mile away, if any of the smugglers were watchful at this hour. The bulk of the cliff was limestone, with occasional outcrops of granite. Durell went first, with Luk and his soldier coming after, a bit more slowly. His first survey found no convenient cranny that might loosen a rockslide onto the road below. He moved to the right, following a line of scrub, and presently saw a bulging overhang

211

that looked like a possibility. There seemed to be no way to get to the underside. He quartered back and up, motioning Luk to follow, and then worked his way down a chute formed by rainwater. It was still wet and slippery, and the going was treacherous. There would be no way to save himself if he fell. Once, the pack of explosives on his back snagged on a ragged bush, and he had to pause, frozen, and work his arm up and back until he found the strap and broke off the twig that held him momentarily a prisoner.

"My man says to the left," Major Luk whispered. "Over there."

"I see it."

The soldier behind Luk was breathing heavily with fright. His eyes gleamed white in the moonlight as they clung to the face of the cliff. All at once his face disappeared and he gave a low, strangled cry. Durell moved to the left and peered down in the faint light. The Thai's brown face was upturned, alarm struggling with a grin, only ten feet below the great bulge of rock that overhung the road.

"I am all right," the man said.

He stood on a ledge under the rock outcrop, breathing hard, but quite safe. Durell carefully lowered himself to join the soldier. The place was a natural.

"Let's get to work," he said.

There were crannies and cracks for planting the explosive in abundance. If everything worked, the charge could drop half the cliff down on the road, blocking the pass. Luk and his man were efficient, but it was Durell who placed the charges and did the wiring. The work took less than fifteen minutes, now that they had found the proper spot. The moon began to set over the dark mountains to the west, as they climbed back up, unreeling the wire behind them. On the ledge outside their cave, Durell checked the batteries, but left the wires unconnected to the detonator. His left leg ached again from the long, dangerous climb, and he accepted a cup of tea from Kem gratefully.

"I have been talking to the *bhikkhus*," Kem said quietly. The eight men now sat in a row, their backs to the wall of the cave, watching Durell as he drank the tea. Their faces all looked alike; they were equally poor and ascetic looking. "The holy men," said Kem, "have decided to help us in any way they can."

"Benjie hasn't come back?"

"I have learned where she is. And the matter of the money – it was all a mistake. Both of the Slocums seem to be innocent."

Mike came hobbling from the back of the cave. His round face was sunken in the two

213

hours Durell had been out on the cliff, and there were red lights far back behind his eyes. Hostility made an electric aura around him, thick enough to touch and taste.

"Are the charges set, Cajun?"

"All set, Mike."

"I hope we mash every one of those bastards."

"We'll do the best we can."

"You didn't look for Benjie?"

"I'm going to, now."

"You have a hell of a set of priorities, Cajun. The job always comes first, doesn't it? You don't give a damn what might have happened to my sister, do you?"

"Do *you?*"

"I owe her plenty. I owe her an effort to get her away from Uva Savag, that's for sure."

Durell looked at Kem. The monk nodded, his eyes obscure with thoughts of his own. Durell said, "Tell me about it, Flivver."

The monk pointed out and below. "She is down there."

A Missa man, Kem said, a refugee from Xo Dong, had come up to the cave while Durell and Major Luk were out on the cliff with the explosives. He was the son of Gujiwandara, the headman, and he had come for the money.

"He knew about it?" Durell asked.

"It is just as Mike said," the monk replied. He smiled at Slocum. "It was the squeeze money collected from the villagers for the Muc Tong. And then the head man decided not to pay it. When the Muc Tong came to the village, he knew Mike would get out, and he hid the money in Mike's pack. Now he wants it back, in his father's name."

"But why did Benjie take it?" Mike asked angrily. "And where is she?"

The Missa said he had seen the *fahrang* woman in the caravan camp. Mike drew a long, angry breath and started to charge the man with lying, then he looked at Durell.

"Okay, so they caught her. She's been turned inside out by all this, Cajun. By you, Sam. It's your fault, if they got her. If it wasn't for my stupid ankle, I'd go down there after her. I hate to think of what those people may do to her."

"Take it easy, Mike."

The Missa man again asked for his money. Kem spoke to him quietly, promising to get it back. Then he looked at Durell. "It is up to you, Sam. But perhaps I can help."

"With your eight old men? Against three hundred?"

"They are *bhikkhus*. They are holy men. They are not afraid. And the caravan men are mostly Buddhist, or superstitious, at any rate."

Mike said, "If we don't get her back, and they take her with them through the pass when they move at dawn, she'll be killed with the rest of the smugglers. Which means you can't set off the charges, Cajun. You'd be murdering her."

"I must," Durell said.

"You'd kill her, too?"

Durell said, "We'll get her out."

"And if you can't?"

"Major Luk will detonate the charges, whether we come back or not."

Mike said, "You're going down there, too?"

"I have to," Durell said.

There was still an hour before dawn when they came to the river bank across from the enemy camp. Durell was grateful for the long watch he had kept on the place that afternoon, spotting the trucks and jeeps and donkey corral, the guard tents and the bunker. The river was shallow here, filled with flat rocks that made easy stepping-stones. The camp slept. The cooking fires had died down, making only dull red embers in the dark hour before sunrise. The moon was down, the skies had cleared, and only starlight glimmered on the surface of the river.

Durell carried the AK-47 he had taken from the guard up the river at the ford. Kem and his eight old men refused to carry any guns at all, except for long staves cut from tree limbs on their way down from the cliff. For some moments, they stood behind tall bamboo that screened them from anyone who might be awake across the river. The caravaneers were secure in their sense of immunity. A few lamps glowed in tents about two hundred yards downstream, and the shadow of a picket moved near the animal corral. A man in a Pathet Lao outfit stood in front of the hidden bunker, beyond the leaning, rickety houses on the river bank. To the left, the glow of a cigarette showed where a mechanic tinkered with a truck engine. The click of his wrench on metal, the sleepy grunt of a donkey, were the only sounds above the quiet purling of the river moving on its rocky bed.

"Your *bhikkhus* know what to do?" Durell asked.

Kem nodded. His dark eyes gleamed with excitement. "They say it is their duty to wipe out evil. They say that meditation may be good for their souls, but what of the souls of the unfortunate criminals over there, who

217

should be assisted in making merit for their next incarnation? Otherwise they may live again only as pigs and dogs and spiders, or worse."

The eight old men began a low, humming chant as Kem spoke, and several of them began clicking beads and prayer wheels as they tucked up their tattered robes and waded out into the stream, brandishing their sticks. For long seconds, nothing happened. No one noticed them.

"Go on, Kem," Durell said.

"I will stay with you. I may be more helpful."

"But those old fellows may be killed."

"They will not be harmed."

The oldest monk began a ululating cry that pierced sharply through the darkness. He was halfway across the river before someone shouted querulously in the caravan camp. The shout was taken up by others, and lights began to bloom here and there among the tents and leaning houses on the opposite bank. Kem started forward, and Durell caught his arm.

"Wait. Let them get into the camp."

An uproar began like the slow, seething churn of a giant sea coming in to shore. More lights flashed on, and a warning shot was fired, and men began tumbling sleepily from wherever they happened to be. The old *bhikkhus* did not pause or hesitate. Their chanting became shouts of rage, and as the first caravaneers ran toward them, yelling warnings, they laid about them sturdily with their staves, whacking and thrusting and cracking the smugglers across their heads and shoulders.

Kem chuckled. "Watch."

In the first fury of the monk's sudden onslaught, the caravan men fell back, astonished. There were some shouted orders from their leaders, and more lights came on, in one of the houses directly in front of the bunker that Durell watched. The smugglers grew in numbers as more and more woke up, but no shots were fired. The old men continued their chanting and shrieking progress up the main camp street, heading away from the bunker, where several men, two in Pathet Lao outfits and another in a Thai uniform, came out and shouted angrily. A lamp was smashed by one of the monks' sticks, a smuggler howled as a second stave cracked him across the scalp. Durell could not guess what the *bhikkhus* were shouting, but their tones were those of sharp reprimand and anger. In less than a minute, they seemed to be swallowed up by a growing circle of the caravan men, none of who dared to touch the old men; nor did they try to stop their progress. Like a flood, the men of the camp moved away from the bunker area across the river from Durell and Kem.

"Now we can go, Flivver."

Durell stood up and ran, crouching, into the stream. Most of the lights in the camp were to the left, surrounding the onslaught of the angry old men. No one stood on guard across the river. Durell dashed through the cold water with all his speed, and threw himself to the bank under the dark shelter of a stilted house. Kem splashed down after him, laughing softly.

"Ah, this is something these old men will always remember. A joy to their waning years."

"If they're not murdered."

"Buddha will watch over them."

Durell crawled under the house, through mud and weeds, holding the AK-47 out of the wetness. So far, he saw no hint that Benjie Slocum was anywhere in the camp, captive or otherwise. Kem breathed lightly beside him. The shadows under the house were filled with debris, odorous and malignant, which Durell did not care to identify. He crawled forward until he could see the main street of the camp. He was about thirty yards from the bunker. He did not know how deep or elaborate its construction might be, or how many men might be posted inside. He wondered if there might be another exit. There often was an escape hole from these places, when the enemy had time to construct them. But the dark line of foliage across the dusty trail hid any hope of finding it. He would have to go in the front way.

The sounds of rioting in the camp increased. Fires sprang up, and now there was angry shouting between two factions of the caravan men – those who considered the old *bhikkhus* holy, if mad, to be treated gently; and those more hardened types who would just as soon cut them all down for disturbing their sleep with their religious fanaticism. It would be touch and go, Durell thought. In either case, the issue would be decided in a few more minutes. There was no time to lose.

He touched Kem's shoulder and got up and ran in a crouch across the road toward the bunker. A single guard was turned the other way, watching the commotion that spread up and down the trail among the trucks and jeeps. The man went down with a single blow, and Durell caught him and lowered him silently to the ground outside the bunker entrance. A rude plank door had been built, covered with pieces of sod. He pulled it open, his gun ready. Faint light came from inside, down a flight of steps cut in the hard, dry ground.

"Stay on watch out here, Kem," he said quietly.

The monk's fingers twitched. "I used to like a good fight, in my college days. You know that I was boxing champion of my class at Williams."

"Just hope you don't have to do anything."

Durell went down the earthen stairs. There was a large bunkroom, with planked walls and teak posts holding up the ceiling. An electric battery lamp lit up the disheveled place. It smelled like an animal's lair. Cans of food were strewn about, empty and battered and rusty. A timbered doorway led him on, across the guard room. Sharp and angry voices came from within. Durell paused, saw a wooden case shoved under one of the lower bunks, and crouched, never taking his eyes from the inner door. He felt within the box. Grenades. He took one, saw it was a Russian GK-51, anti-personnel type. It felt solid and heavy in his hand.

As he straightened, an officer in a Thai-type uniform came hurrying from the inner

222

room of the bunker. His surprise was brief. Durell hit him with the butt of his rifle, and sent him sprawling across the bunkroom. But the man's mouth was open, yelling an alarm, seeing what he thought was a half-breed, strange Chinese. Durell's make-up was still intact. Durell hit him again, but now there was a commotion from inside the bunker, and although he had knocked out the officer, there was no longer the element of surprise in his favor as he pushed quickly down a wooden-shored tunnel to the inner quarters.

"Hold it," he said. "Don't move."

General Savag was there. And two officers in black Pathet Lao uniforms. One of them wore steel-rimmed glasses. The other was older and bald. Between them sat Benjie Slocum.

They were seated at a long plank table, in the glow of a fading battery lantern, and on the table between them was the money Benjie had taken from Mike. There was a bruise on Benjie's forehead, her hair was tumbled down around her face, and her hands were tied behind her back. Her shirt had been torn, exposing a long scratch across her shoulder and more bruises on her arms and chest. Her eyes were dull and defeated. She did not seem to recognize Durell as he filled the low doorway to the command room.

Savag started to lurch from his chair, then halted halfway to his feet as he looked into the muzzle of Durell's rifle. The other two men, the Pathet Lao, stood silently, and a fourth, a man of indeterminate origin, perhaps Viet or Thai, did not move from his position in a corner. He had been smoking a cigarette, and now he dropped it and crushed it out and smiled and said in English:

"So this is the American imperialist spy? The one you told us about, General?"

"He is the one. A madman." Savag's eyes were red with fury. His mouth looked wet. "It seems I have been betrayed." He looked at Durell from black, slanted eyes that were utterly venemous. "Was it Major Luk? The man has foolish ideals. Perhaps you have such ideals, too. But money can change things, eh?"

"Shut up," Durell said. He glanced at the girl. "Benjie?"

She drew a shuddering breath. "I've been stupid, Sam."

"Did you tell them anything?"

"N-no. They tried – they beat me – and threatened me."

"How did they get you?"

"I – I thought I could make a deal. To save Mike. I wasn't sure – I thought he was with them. I don't know. I've been mixed up since you – since we ..."

"All right," Durell said. "Can you stand up?"

"They hurt me, but –"

"Try," he urged.

She wavered to her feet, then fell against the table. The two Pathet Lao did not move to help her. Her hands were still manacled behind her back. Durell said to Savag, "Get those cuffs off her."

"Do it yourself," Savag snarled.

"If I have to take the keys," Durell said, "you'll be a dead man, General. You're as good as dead now. You're a traitor, conspiring with insurgents, taking bribes from smugglers, betraying your country. Unlock Miss Slocum's cuffs."

Durell's voice was quiet, but Uva Savag saw something in his face that convinced him. He got up reluctantly from behind the table, and Durell saw that he wore a holstered revolver.

"Put your weapons on the table. All of you. Don't hold me up too long."

Savag did as he was told. His round, cruel face was covered with sweat. His thick mouth drooped in sullen hatred. The two Pathet

Lao also did as ordered. The other man, apparently the caravan smuggling chieftain, was another matter.

"You will never get away alive," he said. "I see you have a grenade. Will you pull the pin and kill us all – you and the girl, too? I doubt it. But perhaps we can come to an arrangement. You are a chivalrous man, it seems. You came to save the girl. We have no need of her. You may take her. We are not interested in her. We are not interested in you. You can do us no harm. You may take the girl and go."

"You're not concerned about your opium and heroin?"

"You cannot stop us there."

"I suppose not." Durell pretended to think it over. "I want General Savag, though. I'm taking him as a prisoner back to Bangkok."

Savag laughed sourly. The two Pathet Lao smiled. The one with the glasses moved his head and the light splintered off the round lenses. The caravan man said, "That is no deal."

"I insist."

"That is too bad."

The man was fast. Durell never saw where the knife came from until it already had left the man's hand. It flashed in the light of the

226

battery lamp, and then shattered on the barrel of Durell's gun. He fired once, a short burst that knocked the caravan leader back into a bloody heap in a corner of the bunker room. The air smelled of cordite, echoed with the explosions. No one else moved, until the bald Pathet Lao smiled briefly and took a cigarette from a pack on the table. No one turned to look back at the dead man in the corner.

"Let's go, Benjie. Pick up the money."

"Sam –"

"Don't waste time. General Savag, come with us."

The Pathet Lao with the cigarette said, "Go, General. We will get to you easily. Have no fear."

"I am not afraid of this – this –" General Savag snarled. "But we are allies. Friends. We have done business together. This man cannot be trusted not to put a bullet in my head." He looked bitterly at Durell. "You will die very badly, American. I will see to it, personally. I shall think of very exquisite ways for you to die."

"On your feet, General."

He let the stocky Mongol go by him, then urged Benjie out into the bunker corridor. The two Pathet Lao still sat at the table. Durell backed out, taking their revolvers

227

with him. He gave one to Benjie, who took it with limp, nerveless fingers.

Durell closed and locked the door to the command room, then turned quickly to Savag. "You first. Don't try anything foolish, General."

"You will never escape."

"But we'll try, General."

Kem was waiting nervously outside the dugout. His face reflected relief as he saw Durell and Benjie climb up the bunker steps. He showed no surprise at seeing General Savag in the lead, his hands clasped behind his neck.

Some of the uproar in the camp, caused by the eight old *bhikkhus,* had died away. What commotion was left was at the far end of the road, among the trucks and jeeps. Practically every man in the caravan had gathered there. But as Durell urged his little party toward the river, four of the caravan men came trotting back, apparently to report to the bunker. One of them shouted and raised his gun, and Durell fired a burst from the AK-47 over his head. The caravan men scattered, but the alarm was out. For a moment, the whole camp paused, as the sound of the shots echoed back and forth from the hills. Then whistles blew and more men yelled and the first four came on toward the line of houses on the river bank, careful and purposeful now.

Durell pushed Kem and General Savag into the water. He held Benjie by the hand. Her fingers were cold. There was little to be seen in the predawn darkness. They stumbled and splashed and hurried through the knee-deep shallows. Flares were lit, and a searchlight went on and probed brilliantly against the sky, then began to sweep back and forth across the river. A fusillade of shots whipped over their heads, but Durell did not think they could be seen against the dark bank of the river across the way.

"Stay low, Benjie," he said.

They were halfway over when Savag, sensing desperately that this was his last chance, suddenly broke free and stumbled back toward the caravan's shore.

"Hold it!" Durell shouted.

"You will die!" Savag yelled back.

His stocky figure surged through the water toward what he assumed to be safety. Durell squeezed the trigger. He fired above the man's head, and at the same time, shots answered the muzzle flare of his gun. General Uva Savag was caught in the crossfire. Durell saw the two uniformed

Pathet Lao with automatic weapons, sweeping the surface of the river. Savag fell as if hit by a battering ram, his legs and feet coming up, his arms splayed wide as he was knocked backward. Benjie made a thin sound, and Durell pushed her toward the safety of the foliage on the far bank. Savag fell on his back in the water and his body rolled over twice, then floated face down, moving away with the current.

"Come on," Durell said to Kem.

"It was the Pathet Lao who killed him," the monk murmured.

"Maybe they had their reasons, too."

They splashed and surged toward the opposite bank of the river. Some of the caravan men started in pursuit, but Durell threw the grenade, a little downstream, and the explosion burst thunderously in the night over the water. The enemy turned back. Benjie reached out and helped them out of the water. There were shouts and orders and the caravan men retreated all the way. Lights were on all over the camp now.

"The *bhikkhus*," Kem whispered. "The old men!"

"Here they come," Benjie said, awed.

The tattered old hermits totally ignored the excitement and alarm and gunfire, as they waded solemnly out into the stream after them. They still had their sticks and clubs, and they tucked their dirty robes up over their skinny knees as they forged unsteadily into the current.

One after another, truck motors were being started up at the far end of the camp.

"They're going to leave early," Durell said. "And they'll get through the pass before we can use the dynamite."

"We must wait for the old men."

"You wait. Here. Cover them." Durell thrust his rifle into the monk's unwilling hands. "You can get them back to the cave, Flivver."

"I must not kill," the *bhikkhu* protested.

"You don't have to. Fire high. Just hold them off." Durell turned to Benjie and grabbed her hand. "We have to run."

24

They stumbled, fell, picked themselves up, and ran on again, climbing the painful ascent trail of the cliff. Now and then Durell looked back, holding Benjie's hand, pulling her up with him. The whole camp was a beehive of desperate, frantic activity as the caravan leaders decided to move out ahead of time. He did not know what they suspected, but they were certainly alarmed enough to change their plans. He swore softly as Benjie stumbled and fell again.

"Hurry."

"I can't. They hurt me too much."

"You must. Come along."

"We can't make it. Maybe Mike –"

"We can't count on Mike. Or Major Luk. I have to set that dynamite charge off myself."

"We'll be too late."

"Maybe not."

They kept on climbing. Benjie fell again, dragging him down with her. He pulled her to her feet once more. From a vantage point on the trail, Durell paused to let Benjie catch her breath again. Down along the river below, all had gone quiet again. There was no glimpse to be had of Kem and the eight old *bhikkhus*. He did not know if they had been caught or killed, and he could not think about it now.

The way seemed longer than before. Once, at a fork in the trail, Benjie started the wrong way, and he had to pull her back with him. A few truck motors started down in the camp, their engines racketing back and forth in echoes between the rocky walls of the gorge. They were almost to the ledge that led to the last level near the cave when Durell checked himself and pulled Benjie to a halt. Someone was running toward them. It was Major Luk. Mike Slocum hobbled along behind the Thai.

"They're moving out," Mike exploded. "They're going through the pass ahead of time."

Major Luk said quietly, "And General Savag?"

"Dead," Durell said. "His playmates didn't like to see him go with me – as my prisoner."

"Very good," Luk said. "But now we must hurry."

The first trucks and jeeps of the caravan were already lining up on the trail, and a few had nosed into the mouth of the pass. The headlights flared along the rock walls and glinted on the narrow ribbon the river made as it raced along its restricted bed in the gorge. Overhead, the stars were beginning to fade. A faint wind stirred, bringing with it the smell of morning.

"The *bhikkhus?*" Luk asked.

"Coming after us."

"I am relieved. But we must move quickly."

Durell turned to the exhausted girl.

"Benjie, I want you to take it easy. Come the rest of the way with Mike."

It was going to be tight. Never tighter, he thought. More and more trucks were starting up down there, and the first jeep had rolled into the pass and then halted, waiting for the caravan to form into a convoy line. There was dim shouting, orders yelled, some argument. The voices echoed, as if coming from a far-distant tunnel. Some of the Missa men were standing on the ledge outside the cave they had occupied through the night. They looked uncertain as Durell and the Thai officer ran up the last ascent.

More and more of the caravan crowded onto the trail in the gorge. There were only moments left before they would start rolling for the security of the nearby border. Durell began to limp as his knee acted up again, and he swore softly at the doctor who had assured him that the torn ligament had mended as good as new. For a moment he could not find the detonator, and when he located it, he discovered that the wires he had trailed up the face of the cliff had slipped away and were dangling ten feet below the ledge. The sound of the truck motors made a rising thunder that rolled up from below.

"I'll get it," Major Luk said.

He lowered himself quickly, not careful

now, and swung from a grip on some scraggly shrubs that grew out of a crevice in the rock. He could not reach the wires. His small, lithe figure swung back and forth. The first trucks were now almost directly under them. Durell heard a dim chanting and saw the eight old *bhikkhus*, led by Kem, coming up the trail.

"Major!" he called.

"I can get them."

"Go slow. Go steady."

"Yes."

The Thai's face was upturned for a moment. His hold on the shrub was precarious, his legs dangled out over a thousand feet of black space. He jerked as he urged himself into another swing. His arm came out, his fingers closed on one of the wires, caught it, then lost it. He swung again. The shrub cracked, protesting, came partly loose. This time the Thai's fingers caught both wires and pulled and held them. Major Luk looped the strands around his wrist, tying them in a loose knot with his teeth. His brown face turned up toward Durell.

"I am afraid —"

"Take it easy, now."

"— I cannot climb up."

Durell turned. "Kem!"

"I am here. Buddha smiles on us all."

"Hold on to my ankles. I'm going over for Luk."

"Let me try to do it."

"No. It's my job."

Durell slid on his belly over the lip of the ledge. None of the Missa tribesmen offered to help. Mike and Benjie had not yet reached the cave. The trucks of the caravan were now bunching up below, and the headlights shone with glinting reflections off the rock face on the other side of the gorge. Durell dangled head down on the surface of the cliff. He felt Kem's hands holding his ankles in a tight, numbing grip. He hoped the monk was well braced against his weight. It was dizzying, looking upside-down into the gorge and the river. Major Luk tossed the wires up to him. He caught them, twisted, and passed them back and up to the monk.

"I've got them," Kem said briefly. He added, "I seem to have gotten out of condition."

"Save your breath. Major?"

"Yes?"

"Reach up. Grab my hand."

"The *bhikkhu* cannot support us both."

"He won't have to. There's a grip, just over there. All you need is a lift of twelve inches. I'll do it fast, then let you go. Don't fall."

236

"I hope not."

Durell pulled on the Thai's extended wrist. Major Luk surged up, one hand grabbing desperately for the outcrop of rock that could hold him. When Durell felt his ankles slipping through Kem's fingers above him, he let go of the Thai. Major Luk caught at the rock, held it; he swung, got one leg up, stood flat with his body pressed against the face of the cliff.

"Pull me up," Durell told Kem.

"Is he safe?"

"Yes. Safe."

"A very brave man," the young monk said.

In another moment, Durell and the major stood safely on the ledge outside the cave. The eight old *bhikkhus* now sat all in a row, looking downward at the caravan in the gorge. Their faces were serene, but there were glints of pleasure in their old, wise eyes. Durell knelt and fixed the wires to the detonator. His fingers trembled. He did not want to admit to himself how tired he was, or how close he had come to the end.

Major Luk knelt beside him, breathing quickly and lightly. "I want to thank you."

Durell turned the detonator over to the Thai. "You can blow it, yourself. It's your country, after all."

The Thai grinned. "A pleasure. Now?"

237

"Now," Durell said.

Major Luk slammed down on the plunger.

It began slowly at first. The earth trembled slightly, then the blast hit them, a tremendous thunderclap that echoed deafeningly back and forth between the walls of the gorge. A great spray of rock, earth, and debris shot out from under the heavy bulge of granite midway down the cliff, overhanging the road. The trail was crowded with trucks, jeeps, and men while great boulders shot out into space and hung over them. For just an instant, the scene seemed to be frozen. Then the earth shook again, like some monster slowly coming alive, and a heavy rumbling began and grew louder and heavier as the rockslide started down. The noise was overwhelming. Dust boiled up across the pass, and blocked the view. Durell could barely see the caravan lights through it, and then all the lights were obscured by the grinding, churning, roaring mass of the landslide. It seemed to go on forever. The Missa tribesmen on the ledge outside the cave cowered back with shouts of fear. The eight old *bhikkhus* did not move. It seemed to Durell that he could hear their chanting through the tumult, but he could not be sure. He saw that Kem had joined them, and the line had now become nine men.

The taste and smell of dust and grit touched Durell. The earth continued to shake. For a few moments, he did not know if the whole cliff would go down, taking them all with it. He could see nothing of the river below. Then, very slowly, the landslide died away and ended.

Someone took his hand and stood beside him. It was Benjie. "Sam . . ."

"It's over."

"Are they all dead?"

"I think most of them got away. But the trail is blocked, and most of their trucks are buried. And the river is dammed up. Look."

There was a faint gray light in the sky now. It would soon be dawn. Down below, clouds of dust slowly drifted away in the morning breeze. Where the trail had been beside the river there was now a huge mass of jumbled rock and earth and broken trees. The road was gone. The river swirled muddily behind the great barrier, slowly forming a large pond, and then a lake. It would overflow the dam in a day or two, but by then it would not matter. The caravan was destroyed.

Major Luk drew a deep breath and sat down beside him. The Thai's face was drawn and haggard, but he looked happy.

"It is done. The smugglers have been dealt a blow from which they cannot recover for

239

at least a year. All the money they would have collected – which would have gone mostly to finance the insurgent army – is lost. Next year the hill people might have another crop of poppies for them, but by then, we hope, the entire organization should be in our net." He paused and looked at Durell. "You have done your job well, sir."

Durell said, "It's not finished yet."

25

Durell said, "You're shivering, Benjie."

"I can't help it."

"We have lots of time yet."

"Yes. It's good to be alone with you again. I'm grateful to you. I don't know how I could have stood it, if you – if we – had found that Mike was guilty. I couldn't bear the thought that he'd gone so bad that he was a traitor, selling out to the Muc Tong."

"Mike's all right. He just has to be allowed to be his own man. The Missa people will bring him along soon."

She was silent for a moment, then said, "Sam, did it mean anything?"

240

"I don't know. We just have to do what we can."

"I mean, about you and me..."

"I don't know about that, either."

Benjie said, "You say it isn't over for you yet. What do you mean by that?"

"Unfinished business."

"I'm worried about it. I'm worried about you. I don't think I could stand it, always wondering where you were, what you were doing, who was trying to kill you, or –"

"Don't," he said.

"It's an old story with you, isn't it? No permanent entanglements. No involvements. Like for the moment."

"Perhaps."

"Do you like it that way?"

"No. But I chose it, and it's now the only way I know. It's too late to go back."

"You can't get out of the spook business?"

"No."

"You mean you don't want to."

"That's right."

They were waiting in the tumbledown drying shed of the abandoned tea plantation, next to Benjie's Apache plane. It was almost noon, and the air was hot and still and lifeless. Birds and insects made the only sounds to be heard. It had taken most of the morning to make their way through a hostile, confused countryside, past the ruins of Xo Dong and up over the mountain to the terraced slopes of the tea farm. Mike and Major Luk were not far behind them, but they had separated for safety, the easier to make their way around the *wiengs* that were beehives of angry activity since the explosion and the landslide. The caravan men who survived were on the hunt, too, and they had to be avoided. Their thirst for vengeance made the prospect of a quick death a certainty, if they were caught.

"Sam?"

"We'll wait until noon," he said.

"I couldn't leave Mike here."

"He'll be along by then."

"And if he isn't?"

"I told you. Unfinished business in Bangkok."

She rolled over on the straw, her body close to him, and stretched, touching the length of him with her hand. "Sam, we may never be alone like this again."

"That's probably true."

"It was beautiful, before. Wonderful, the first time."

"Benjie, don't just feel grateful –"

"It isn't only that. You changed me."

Insects hummed in the quiet, fragrant shadows of the tea shed. Beyond the open side, past the plane, he could see the landing strip and the trail that led away over the mountain, away from the plantation back to Xo Dong. A bird whipped across the terraces, bright red and green, long tail streaming behind its darting flight. Benjie's mouth was soft and warm and yielding. She shivered again, but she was not cold. She held him tightly, pulling him toward her, demanding him.

"Sam, make love to me. Please."

"Yes."

They waited until ten minutes after noon, and then he saw Major Luk and his troopers, and Kem and Mike coming up the trail. Mike had to be supported with an arm around the monk's shoulders. His face was haggard, bearded and grim. But a flash of his irrepressible spirit showed in his quick laugh as he sagged against the plane.

"Good. Oh, very good. Benjie, you're a wonder."

"That's the first nice thing you've said to me in years," Benjie told him.

"Maybe I never appreciated you before. Or saw you like this."

"Have I changed? I haven't changed," she said.

"I think you have. And so have I."

243

Kem coughed softly. The *bhikkhu* looked more bedraggled than ever, but his black eyes were shy. "Sam, we have been talking. Major Luk will report to his station, at the military security post near here. I know there is a place in the plane for me, and for Mike, too. But I do not wish to go back with you to Bangkok. Have I fulfilled my end of our bargain, the one we made so long ago?"

"I think so."

"Then I am free of my promise?"

"If you wish," Durell said. "Washington would like to keep you with us, though."

The monk shook his shaven head and smiled. "I have made much merit for my soul these days with you. I am free again. My vows are completed. And I would make more merit for my spirit's future, by staying here."

Durell guessed what Kem had in mind. "With your eight old men? You said they were ready to choose another for this year."

"That is correct. I would like to stay with them, if I may, and meditate and pray with them."

"If that's what you want, Flivver."

"My name is Kem Pasah Borovit, of the Sangha."

"Yes. That's right."

"Then," said the monk quietly, "I will help you roll out the plane and see you off safely for Bangkok."

26

The tub was long and wide, built of imported Italian marble; the water was hot and steamy and fragrant with scented oil that the hotel attendant had sprinkled in it. Durell had had several bourbons on the rocks sent up from the bar, had eaten a dinner of spiced and curried Indonesian *rijstaffel*, and the hotel doctor had daubed ointments and antiseptic on the various nicks and bruises he had suffered all over his body. He had been shaved by the barber sent up from the lobby, while he sipped the cold bourbon and thought about the rest of the matters he had to attend to in Bangkok.

He had a plane ticket back to Washington in the morning. It was now eight o'clock in the evening, and he felt there was no hurry about anything. She would come to him. She had to come to him. He had chosen the new hotel in the heart of the city, and then gone to the Embassy and showed his card and had been taken to the communications room where he spent half an hour encoding his report to General Dickinson McFee, the boss of K Section.

He remembered her eyes, the soft and feminine texture of her face, the slim, lithe body, the way she moved and spoke. She would be here. He had left the hotel door unlocked. There was nothing to do but wait. It was something he had to do, and this time he didn't mind the waiting.

He was a little worried about Jimmy James. He had telephoned the K Section Control man's house, remembering the plush appointments of his home, and his elegant manner of living. There had been no answer. He had tried several times, listening to the telephone ring, and the hotel had cooperated by sending around a messenger with a note. The messenger reported the door locked and the windows dark and the cats in their cages. But no one was in the house. He had left Durell's note tacked to the front door, as instructed.

In the tub, feeling the balm of the hot water soak into his bruised ribs, sensing the warmth of the bourbon in his belly, Durell did not worry too much about the elegant James D. James. Benjie and Mike Slocum had left him in a taxi at the hotel and gone to their house on the riverfront that Benjie had built some years ago. Durell had never seen it. Their parting had been brief, hurried by weariness after the flight down from Xo Dong, a bit strained by the let-down of the task being done and over with, the thing now relegated to the past, to the dossiers and the files. Mike had blathered on a bit about another job for K Section, but his eyes admitted to Durell that he was finished with such work for Durell, and he would have to look elsewhere for the risks and excitement he seemed to need. He was more than a little drunk when they had landed, having hit another of his bottles of Mekong whiskey pretty hard, all during the flight back.

She had to come soon, Durell told himself.

But maybe she wouldn't.

Maybe she was too smart for it.

Still, she had to know. She couldn't just let it end this way. She would come and ask and do what she could, questioning and trying to pry him open to satisfy herself, to make herself feel secure again.

He had made his trail plain enough. The switch from his old hotel was open and obvious. His brief journey to the Embassy had not been secret. He had left an obvious trail for anyone to follow.

He did not feel tired now. He was anxious to get it over with. He wanted to go home.

Then she was there.

"Miss Ku."

"Hello, Cajun."

"I've been expecting you."

"I thought you would be."

"Come in, if you like."

"I don't mind."

"Would you get me the towel?"

"No need for the towel."

Smiling, she stood in the bathroom doorway, small, beautiful, and exquisite in a shocking pink silk *cheongsam,* an ivory comb in her high-piled, jet-black hair, her smooth thigh showing through the slit dress. Her mouth was full and fresh and ripe and inviting. He had not heard her come in through the door. He had left it unlocked while he waited, soaking in the tub, and he was a little troubled that she could have come in so silently, almost, but not quite, surprising him. He worried for a moment that he might be getting a bit slower, losing the snap and alertness that was needed in his business, if you wanted to stay alive. Then he shrugged off the momentary unease and enjoyed the beautiful, infinitely alluring image she made as she paused in the doorway. Jimmy James had, without a doubt, excellent taste.

"Are you alone?" she asked.

"Quite alone."

She bit her ripe underlip. "I thought Jimmy might be here with you. Reports, and all that."

"I don't know where Jimmy is," Durell said. "He seems to have disappeared."

She smiled. "Ah, yes."

"You don't know where he is?"

"No. May I pour you another drink, Cajun?"

"Please."

"Stay where you are," she said. "You poor man. You must be exhausted. Jimmy never envied you field agents. Too strenuous and dangerous a life for him, he said. He loved the desk work, the codes and the planning and all the fine litle arrangements to be made, before a man like you went off on the – the hunt, as he put it."

"You talk of Jimmy as if he were dead and gone."

"Poor Jimmy," she said.

"Is he dead?"

"Did you know he was almost impotent?"

"No. Is he dead?"

"He's disappeared."

"Truly?"

"I do not know where he is."

"Doesn't that bother you, Miss Ku?"

"Oh, I know *you* would come back. I was not worried."

"I should think you'd be worried, though," he said.

"About what?"

"I thought you'd like to know about General Uva Savag," he said. "Your very close and intimate – and not so impotent – friend."

She wasn't as good as she would have liked to be. For a moment her great black eyes showed puzzlement, and her lips slowly parted and he could hear the small sound of her breath between her tiny white teeth. Her arched brows slowly went up in inquiry. She took a tentative step through the bathroom doorway from where she had been standing. Durell chose that moment to lean forward in the tub and open the drain and then he stood up, reaching for the towel.

She said, "My good friend, Uva Savag?"

"I saw you with him in Chiengmai."

She looked prettily puzzled as she shook her head. "Oh, no. Impossible. You must have been mistaken. No, no. I see what the trouble is. I sensed the moment I came here that you are angry with me. Is that it? But you simply made a silly mistake. I was – I was Jimmy's, as much as he could demand of me. Which wasn't very much, poor man. He put on such airs, Jimmy did. He liked to exhibit me, as if I were his personal possession. It was very difficult for me, you understand. I am a normal young woman. When I saw you – when I see you now –" She faltered and blushed.

Durell faced her at the other end of the large bathroom, toweling himself. His eyes never left the girl's lovely face. She flushed deeper. Maybe it was sincere, he thought. On the other hand, she knew what she was doing.

"Uva Savag was a pretty old man, too, for a girl like you," he said.

"Uva isn't –" She paused and laughed. "I don't know what you are talking about, Cajun."

"I'm saying that maybe Jimmy James and General Uva Savag were working it together. Using you, perhaps, poor Miss Ku, while they raked in fabulous profits from the drug syndicate, from the caravans, from the village heroin refineries up in the Golden Triangle. Using military transport to get the heroin into the pipelines going to American forces and American ports for distribution throughout the U.S., killing youngsters, making them soft and weak so that, one day,

251

one month, one year, America will be easy pickings for your Peking leaders. I saw one of Savag's checkpoints, or collection points – an abandoned barracks off the military highway north of Bangkok."

"You confuse me," she whispered. She had turned a bit pale now. "Are you talking about Jimmy and Uva, or me?"

"Maybe all of you."

"Not I," she said. She looked at him, weighing his naked body as a prospective purchaser might consider a prize stud animal. There was a note of wonder and perplexity in her voice. "I do not excite you, Cajun?"

"No."

"Could I? I would like – you and I . . ."

"Maybe. Do you think I'm right? Was James in with Savag? Was James the dragon head of the syndicate? It makes sense, you see. He used you, Ku, for his messages. Didn't you realize what it all added up to?"

"No, I did not." She showed some excitement and eagerness when she spoke now. She came all the way into the bathroom and picked up his towel and began helping him towel away the water on his body, making little sounds of sympathy over the scars and bruises that she found. The water went out of the tub with a final gurgle. "You

are right. You are so clever! Why did I not
see before how I was being used? Of course,
it all makes sense now. I – I was afraid to
admit it, even to myself – about running
errands for Jimmy to General Savag.
Sometimes I thought it was strange –
carrying money, carrying packages. But your
business is a strange one, anyway, is it not?
All secrecy and no explanations unless
absolutely essential – and then, Jimmy's
explanations never quite held the ring of
truth in them. And how did he live so
extravagantly? You have no idea how much
it cost him to live in the style he demanded.
Of course, he was getting paid off, helping
to protect and run the Muc Tong's drug
caravans. Yes, of course. And you can
unmask him now. He knows you have come
back safely. And suddenly he has disappeared! He has utterly vanished. But
perhaps, one day, you will find him. I am
sure you will. I admire you. I think you can
do anything."

"Doesn't it bother you?" he asked quietly.

She was puzzled. "What should bother
me?"

"About Uva Savag. He's dead."

"Savag is dead?" She looked blank,
rejecting his words.

"That's what I said."

Her voice was shaken. "You killed him?"

"Not I. Not actually. I caused it, but I didn't pull the trigger personally. He tried to escape from me. Two Pathet Lao officers who were with him did it. They didn't want him to talk, I suppose. I guess they thought they still had you for their major contact here in Bangkok, you as their dragon head."

"Me? You suspect me?"

"You're not too distressed because Savag is dead," he said. "You knew it before you walked in here. You've had time to adjust to the fact that you don't have to go on being his mistress any more, haven't you?"

"Cajun," she said, "I thought you and I had agreed that it's Jimmy you want."

"I didn't agree to anything."

"It's me? You think it's me?"

"I know it was you. It was the other way around from the diagram you're trying to draw for me. Not you working for Jimmy. But James working for you – willingly or not, knowingly or not. He would have hated the thought of losing you. You could manipulate him easily enough. You're a very pretty dragon head, Miss Ku Tu Thiet; but you're going to jail. You're going to court. You're going to be sentenced. I think you're going to die."

She stood very close to him, very still, her

breathing quick and shallow. Her perfume was delicate, exquisite. He could read nothing in her lovely, large black eyes. Her ripe mouth looked wet; she had her underlip caught between her small white teeth.

"Very well. I will confess," she whispered. "Yes, I am guilty. I knew about the caravans, the refineries, the dope smuggling. I know all about it. But it was as part of Jimmy's organization. I am a simple girl. Most of my life I have been alone, and had to struggle and scheme for myself, and my livelihood depended on the job with Jimmy. What was I to do? I was innocent enough. I knew he worked for your K Section, as Bangkok Central, and I learned a bit of this and a bit of that, and I really had no idea, in the beginning, that Jimmy's work with the Muc Tong was not part of his orders from American intelligence. How could I know otherwise? It is a strange, upside-down world you work in. Jimmy gave me orders, and I obeyed them. He was kind enough to me. I took orders from him, since he knew things about me – about my past. He took me in, and I was very grateful, and I was willing to do anything he asked of me." She paused suddenly. Her eyes were filled with tears. She looked very beautiful and totally helpless. "Do you believe me, Cajun?"

"Go on," he said quietly. He could feel her warmth against his body.

"But you must believe me!"

"Not yet."

"I can prove everything I say!" she cried.

"How?"

"I have the proof. I have the evidence. But you must help me. I am afraid of everything. The Muc Tong, you, Jimmy. I am afraid to go to court or to prison. I come from a family –" She paused and swallowed painfully. Her hands were flat on his chest. "They must not know about me. Please, Cajun. I'll do anything. Anything, you understand?"

"I understand better than you imagine."

"I have the proof, Sam. But first – you're tired, you've had a terrible time, and I want to show you –"

She stepped back, and with a quick, smooth gesture that bespoke a certain expertise, she unzipped her *cheongsam* and stepped out of it. Her body gleamed as flawlessly as a pearl. She smiled suddenly, secretly, her eyes looked up at him as she took his hand. "Come. I have the papers in the other room, in my handbag. I put it down when I came in, in the bedroom."

He let her go first, wrapping the towel around his waist. Her body was delicate, yet womanly, shimmering before him. He sat down on the edge of the bed, the towel still around him. Ku went to a table near the door, where she had placed a large yellow handbag of rough linen; she rummaged in it for a few moments, took out a fat manila envelope, and turned to face him, holding the papers in both hands close to her breasts. He made no effort to rise from the bed.

"It is all here, Sam. All the proof you need. You will not doubt me, after you read it all."

"Put it down," he said.

"Don't you want to read it now?"

"Later."

She brought both the handbag and the envelope with her as she came to the bed. Her body moved like warm silk against him. She had the technique of a professional courtesan. Her breath was perfumed. Her mouth was soft and warm and clinging against his.

"Oh, Sam, it has been so long . . ."

"You've had Jimmy."

"I told you about Jimmy. Something was wrong with him."

"Do you have any idea where he might be?"

"He's run away, of course. Do we have to talk about him?"

"He's part of my job," Durell said.

"Must you always think of your job – even now?"

"Do you think he's dead?"

"I do not know." She was not interested. Her black eyes were veiled as she moved her hands over him. He thought briefly of Benjie; he held an image of her as she swam in the little river at Xo Dong, flickering in the back of his mind. She sensed his detachment and pulled him down upon her with a small sound of impatience.

"Listen . . ." he began.

"Please, Sam." She kissed his mouth, his eyes, his chest. "Please."

"Tell me about General Uva Savag."

"I did tell you. Jimmy used me as a messenger to him, that's all."

"How long were you and he lovers?"

She looked at him with wide, startled eyes. "Jimmy and me?"

"Savag and you."

"But I – it was not that way –"

"Yes, it was. You and Savag. Double dragon heads. You were the brains, really. You organized it. You used Jimmy to run the Muc Tong's drug caravans. Savag had the military control of the districts and he let the caravans go through safely, while you told him how to do it and when, to avoid the

258

American and Thai government's security plans to interfere."

Her body went rigid. "I thought you believed me, Sam. How can you even think of it, at a moment like this?"

"Did you kill Jimmy," he asked softly, "after you heard I'd come back?"

She didn't move under him. She took one long breath, and her breasts felt soft under his chest. The only light in the room came from the open door to the bath. It touched her thick hair, spread like a fan on the pillow slip, and ran pale fingers along the contours of her flower-petal face. For a long moment she simply lay there, looking up into his eyes. Her hands slowly slid away from his back.

He was ready for her.

He heard the faint click of the clasp as she opened the linen handbag on the bed beside them. He couldn't see it, the bag was down at her side and below his line of vision, but at the instant that he felt the muscular tension in her right arm, he moved, rolling off her and away, turning his head to see the steely flicker of the needlelike knife in her hand.

She was quick and surprisingly strong. The blade came down for his back with tremendous force. Her face was contorted, her mouth open, her tongue wet against her

259

teeth as she struck. He was not quite fast enough. The edge of the blade was like a razor, slicing through the skin on his left arm as it came down. He rolled all the way apart from her, feeling the hot pain of the wound down to his fingertips. The girl made a hissing sound of exasperation as the knife thudded into the bed. Then she rolled away, too, as fast as a cat, her nude body catching the light from the bathroom door. Durell plunged his hand under the pillow and came up with his short-barreled .38 S&W. Ku rolled again, on her knees, and pulled the knife free of the bedding. Her face glared with hatred, her dark hair swung before her eyes as she slashed at him again with feline speed.

He had no choice: he aimed for her shoulder, but she was moving too fast, coming at him across the bed with the blade. The sharp, sudden report of his gun did not make too much noise in the hotel room. A hole appeared between her breasts, and she kept coming forward, falling, her eyes suddenly, wide, blank and empty. The knife caught his forearm again and slashed across the back of his wrist. He caught her as she fell forward, face down.

"Ku? About Jimmy James –"

She made a small sound, a whisper of

breath that escaped from between her white teeth. The knife slid from her hand. Durell swore softly. His arm was bleeding badly. Quietly, he disentangled himself from the girl.

She was dead.

27

Durell went back into the bathroom and washed his arm and took antiseptic ointment from his suitcase and daubed it on and then tore one of his shirts into strips and bandaged his forearm and the back of his wrist, then applied tape to it. It was quiet in the room. No one seemed to have heard the shot he had fired. When he had the bleeding stopped, he dressed, picking a dark suit and another white shirt and a dark necktie. He went to the corridor door and locked it. Ku Tu Thiet's nude body lay like marble across the bed.

The big yellow handbag had fallen off the bed and spilled its contents on the floor – lipstick, comb, coin purse, a currency roll of high-denomination bahts in a man's gold clip that looked as if it might have been Jimmy's, or a gift from Jimmy. He used her Thai silk handkerchief to pick up the bag and open it wide, being careful about it, and unzipped the inner side pocket, which bulged a little. From it he took out two plastic caps like black buttons, about an inch in diameter. He frowned, weighing these in the flowery, perfumed handkerchief, and he wondered what Miss Ku had been doing with plastic explosive. He put the caps in his pocket and opened the manila envelope which she had said held proof of James D. James' involvement with the Muc Tong. He expected to find nothing in it, and he was right. All it contained was a thick, folded wad of yellow typing paper, all blank. It made him feel a little better for what had happened, then.

He picked up Miss Ku's slender little knife and wiped his blood off the blade, using tissue from the bathroom and flushing the bloody paper down the toilet. The knife was a gem, the handle intricately carved with small Thai motifs and with a ruby-like jewel at the top of the gold hilt. He decided to keep it, and slipped it into his jacket pocket, covering the honed steel blade with one of his own handkerchiefs wadded thickly around the razor-like edge.

He did not look at her body again. He

went to the telephone and called the Embassy number and spoke to the communications man who had helped him file his report to Washington. The Embassy man's name was Rogers.

Durell said briefly, "You'll have to call the police, of course. Anonymously, and make it Internal Security. You'll have to wipe my name from the hotel register. Make it look like a lover's quarrel. Put in a fictitious Thai male name for my room. You'll have to use all the squeeze you can, Rogers. It'll cost, but it has to be done."

"What will you be doing?"

"I'm moving out."

"You'd better get over here, Mr. Durell."

"Can't do that, yet. Have you heard from Mr. James?"

"Nothing, sir. Not a word."

"He may be dead," Durell said. "But I've got to look for him."

"Won't that be a bit risky, sir?"

Durell could still smell Miss Ku's perfume in the room. "What isn't risky?" he said softly, and hung up.

Outside the hotel, he took a taxi and told the driver to head for the Chao Phraya River. Traffic was heavy, and he thought he might have done better using a motorized *samlaw*

263

that could weave through the congestion. It was only nine o'clock in the evening.

His left leg ached again, and when they passed an American-type drug store, he told the driver to stop and wait, and he went in and purchased an elastic knee bandage and slipped it on behind the counter. He bought some aspirin, asked the druggist for water, and took three tablets, then returned to the cab. In the back seat, he unwrapped Miss Ku's knife and slipped it into the knee bandage on his left leg. It would not be too easy to get at speedily, but it might still be useful, he thought.

Near James D. James' house, he had the taxi wait, and walked the short distance down the narrow *soi* that led toward the *klong* and the river. The lane was dark, and the adjacent houses behind their private walls looked peaceful and innocent enough. The gate to James' property was not locked. No lights shone from the windows under the wide sweep of gracefully tiled roof. He stopped just inside the gate, in the deep shadow of a tall oleander bush and simply stood and listened and watched. He was filled with a sense of urgency that fought against the need for patience. Through the shadows, it seemed that the ornate front door stood ajar, with a column of darkness just showing where he could look inside. Starlight gleamed on the small brass name plate beside the door. Nothing moved. He heard a boat go by on the *klong*. A radio played Thai ballet music. He did not hear or smell the cats. Their cages across the lawn seemed to be empty. The absence of the cats troubled him.

After a time, he walked through the shadows and reached the overhang of the upturned roof eaves; he approached the door from the side. Nobody stopped or challenged him. He used his fingertips to ease the door all the way open.

There was a spitting sound, a brief yowl, and small feet scampered away into the large living room. The house was black with shadow, silver with reflected light that came through the windows. He saw all of the cats then, small shapes with great eyes shining in the darkness, all watching him. He drew his gun and went all the way in.

Nothing was the same. The place looked as if a wild animal had gone on a rampage through it. The coffee table was smashed, the elegant draperies torn from their brass rods over the windows, pictures pulled down from the wall, cushions ripped open and emptied of their stuffing, the rugs pulled back and hurled to one side. The place was empty. He walked through the forest of overturned furniture, and the cats gathered silently around him, watching. They followed him through the kitchen, and he looked at the open cupboards, the small mountain of utensils piled on the floor, the open oven door. They had even taken the heating elements out of the built-in stove, in their search.

The search was too thorough to have been done quickly. What was done here had taken hours, and they hadn't cared to hide their effort, certainly.

Durell went into the bedroom and saw that the bed had been torn apart, ripped open, the pillows emptied, the wardrobe closets scoured; James' elegant clothing was piled in ripped and crumpled tatters on the floor. He went on into the radio room. The GK transceiver was smashed. The locks on the files were broken, and the dossiers and folders were gone. He made a faint clucking sound, and one of the cats spoke to him in reply and suddenly jumped on his shoulder. He let it stay there. It was the Lilac Point. He spoke to the Siamese quietly, soothing it, and it stopped clawing at his shoulder and let him carry it about.

There would be hell to pay over K Section Central's missing files here in Bangkok. But that was for Washington to worry about.

266

Nowhere was there any trace of personal violence to James himself. Or any trace of James.

In every Central station there was an emergency cache, that followed a world-wide system of coded locations. In James' house in Bangkok, Durell knew, the code was Sigma Fifteen. He went back to the front door, carrying Phan on his shoulder. At the door he faced inward and then paced off fifteen steps along the wall to his left. A couch had stood in front of this wall, but it had been pulled out several feet from the paneled wall and overturned and ripped apart with a large knife, so that the stuffing stood out in great balls and strands, like a man's intestines when his stomach has been ripped open. The thought made him pause. The paneling on the wall was of fine Philippine mahogany, and there had been a picture hanging here. The hook was still in the wood, but the painting had been taken down and the back paper torn off and then thrown across the room. Durell touched the hook, and Phan clawed at his shoulder and murmured. The eyes of the other cats were luminous glowing circlets in the shadowed, silent room.

Durell traced the fine, almost microscopic lines of a small door built into the paneling.

267

He didn't think the emergency cache had been opened, but he went across the room and picked up one of the long brass curtain rods and took the time to bend one end into a hook that would catch the one nailed into the wall that had held the painting.

When he was satisfied, he returned along the wall and flattened against it at the distance of the rod and then maneuvered the brass pole so that it caught on the picture hook. He was eight feet away from the wall safe. His first attempt to pull the door open failed. The Lilac Point jumped from his shoulders with a hissing sound. He waited, watching all the cats, but they did not go out of the room. He tried the rod again, caught it in the hook, and swung it more carefully, pulling it with a sudden yank that all at once released the spring mechanism and opened the door.

The room thundered and shook and lit up with a brief flare of red light. The explosion gushed outward, shooting bits of metal and debris from the square hole in the wall. If he had been standing in front of the little door, he would have had his head blown off.

He coughed from the acrid smoke that filled the house. A window across the room cracked and a large piece of glass slowly slid from the sash and broke on the floor.

The echoes of the explosion seemed endless.

Durell felt in his pocket and took out the two plastic detonator buttons he had found in Miss Ku Tu Thiet's handbag. He tossed them away, and felt even better when he thought of her lying dead in his hotel room.

He wasted no further time in the house. The explosion would surely bring inquiries from neighbors, and eventually the local police.

When he left, he opened the front door wide and urged the cats out ahead of him. They were not reluctant to leave the house now. They scampered out on the lawn, tails erect, and headed for the gate and vanished.

Durell walked back to the taxi.

28

"Benjie?"

"Yo, Sam. You woke me up."

Her voice did not sound sleepy. He said, "Where is Mike?"

"In his bed, where else? I had our doctor come and put a cast on his ankle. It was

269

fractured, actually, so he's laid up for a while. Shall I call him to the phone?"

"No."

She said, "Are you all right?"

"More or less."

"Still working?"

"Trying. Have you had any visitors?"

"Nobody. Like cops, you mean?"

"Like people taking your house apart. Like people coming in to kill you."

"Oh, you and your spook business." She laughed. "Sam – darling? Why don't you come over here and rest for the night?"

"I'd like that."

"Then come on over. Mike is asleep with a sedative. We can – well, I'm wide awake now. I went to sleep thinking about you."

"Benjie, lock your doors. Lock your windows. Stay awake, whether I get there or not."

"You sound strange, Sam. Are you in trouble?"

"No, I'm fine. Just be careful."

"I thought it was all over," she protested. "You aren't really working now, are you? Not really? I thought you were all set to leave tomorrow, and I feel funny about it, your going away on your damned spook business, just when we – when you and I –"

"I'll see you later," Durell said. "Don't open your doors to anyone but me."

"Nobody wants anything from me now," she said. "I don't have anything anyone could possibly want."

"Probably not. But be careful, anyway."

He hung up. The taxi was waiting outside the restaurant where he had made the telephone call. He got in, favoring his bandaged knee, and tried to remember the name of the alley where Uncle Hu lived. It wouldn't come to his mind. He was too tired, he thought. He was pushing himself too far, too fast. But he couldn't stop now. It was the only place he could think of, the only thing he could do next. He told the driver to go across the bridge over the Chao Phraya and directed him to the left, down the narrow street for several blocks. After a short distance he recognized the watergate market, where sampans and barges huddled in dark shadows, and the smells of cooking and marketing vegetables filled the warm night. The poor houses that crowded at the edge of the *klong,* the endless murmur of voices, babies crying, men talking, radios blaring, and the general press of life behind the bamboo-curtained windows, was not the sort of environment that James D. James would have appreciated.

271

Uncle Hu's house, like James' house, was dark and silent when he approached. He remembered the *klong* pit and the tunnel and the *kamoys* who had attacked him here when he had first arrived in Bangkok. Only seventy-two hours had gone by since then. He paused, then crossed the tiny garden with its spirit house on a pole. The bottle of whiskey and the wad of money he had left on the tiny, ornate platform to placate the *phis* and Uncle Hu were gone. He walked on down to the edge of the canal, under the leaning palm trees. The sampan was still there, tied to a tall bamboo pole. A dim light glowed in the tiny cabin up forward.

Durell drew back into the shadows. A boat went by on the canal, its wake made the sampan rock a little at its mooring. Across the canal, he could see the blue flicker of a television set through a window opening on a veranda. A child cried. A woman sang. He felt oppressed both by life and death.

Finally he stepped down onto the sampan. Behind him, Hu's house remained dark and silent. The light boat tipped under his weight as he moved forward among the pots and pans and clay jars and fish nets used by the old Thai in his daily business.

"Uncle Hu?" he called softly.

The old man sat motionlessly in the tiny

cabin, in front of his charcoal stove. His ancient eyes, like a lizard's, were wide open, staring at nothing. For a moment, Durell thought he was dead. Then the old man blinked and slowly lifted a blue china cup of tea to his dry mouth. His gnarled, work-hardened hands trembled slightly.

"Uncle Hu."

"Ah, it is the *fahrang* once again, with his mixed blessings."

"You sound bitter, Uncle."

"Should I not be?" the old man whispered. "My wife Aparsa, the two nephews..."

"Kem is alive and meditating in the mountains."

The old man's eyes blinked again. "You have seen him?"

"He has been very helpful. The debt is discharged."

"Ah."

"Are you all right, Uncle?"

"I am not well. I am lonely. I am thinking of another wife. But you should not come to my house again. You should go away."

Durell felt a shock at the old man's words. It was not in the Thai tradition to be inhospitable, whatever the situation. He stared at Hu's wrinkled face, but he could read nothing in its lined and seamy contours.

273

He smelled the tea, smelled dried fish. The ancient lizard eyes blinked again.

"Go," Hu said.

"I am looking for a man."

"You looked before. You found him."

"A *fahrang*," Durell persisted. "My boss, in a way. His name is James D. James."

"Go away," said Hu.

"Have you seen such a *fahrang?*"

"There is nothing but death here, nothing but desolation in my house. I do not say that it was you who brought it, *Nai* Durell. It is not for me to say that one dies because of another's acts. It is the will of Buddha, and it is sometimes cruel and inscrutable, this work of heaven, and I am not a man who likes to turn the other cheek, as you Christians claim that one must do. I do not see you doing so, in any case. You are all barbarians. And you think that we Thai are barbarians, in our way. We do not understand each other. Go away."

"Have you seen James? Did he come here?"

"Yes."

"When? How?"

"Today. Not long ago. You persist? I have warned you to leave. I have seen too many evil things in my life." The old man sighed and put down his teacup. His twisted hands

274

were steady now. It was as if he had been sitting here on his sampan, not knowing who or what to expect, and now that he saw it was Durell who had come aboard his boat, he felt better. But there was little of this in his brown face and dark old eyes. He said, "I am not alone here. Do you understand?"

"I think so," Durell said.

"There is no help to be had anywhere. A man must gain his own revenge. It is not written that one should act in cruelty or vengeance, but man is what he is, and evil lives in him as well as good, and so he is always torn, first this way and then that, and afterward he does not know what he has done to his soul."

"Is James still here?" Durell asked.

"He came to look for you, and said you were a bad man, a traitor to your country. Or so he thought. He also looked for another *fahrang*, a man named Mike Slocum. He said you had both tried to betray him."

"Where is James now?"

"He is in the *klong* jar pit," said Uncle Hu.

Durell got up and walked to the bow of the sampan, balancing himself against the rocking of the light boat. Lights made ribbons of yellow on the waters of the canal. He looked at the opposite bank of the waterway. The edges of the *klong* were fringed with dense shrubbery and trees, small docks and poles and boats. Life on the *klongs* had a rhythm of its own, a way that was distinct from the rest of the big, sprawling city. He stood for a moment, studying the darkness across the canal. He spotted one man, then another. One wore a pale shirt, and it showed as a light patch against the shrubbery shadows that should not have been there. The other man was careless enough to be smoking a cigarette. The smoker took one last drag that made the end glow red suddenly, and then he flipped the smoke into the water. Durell watched it arc toward him. It fell halfway across the canal, in his direction.

He did not turn as Uncle Hu came out of the sampan cabin. He said, "Is James still alive?"

"I do not know."

"Who put him in the pit?"

"I did. To keep him safe."

"Who is in the house?"

"Chuk."

"Chuk?" Durell stared at the wizened little Thai. "Uncle, how many men does he have with him this time?"

"Six. Possibly seven. I have tried to count them, but I am not sure. They are all armed. They are waiting for you. I do not know why he is certain you would come here, but he is here, waiting."

"Does he know you were waiting for me, too?"

The old man blinked. "They have not troubled me. When I heard them coming, I put *Nai* James in the pit. Then I walked here to my boat for my tea. They have not come to talk to me yet."

Durell looked at the two men across the canal. They had a small boat moored near their watch posts. He scanned the tiny garden of Uncle Hu's house. No other men were visible. So there were four, maybe five in the house, with the fat and vindictive Mr. Chuk. He drew a deep breath. He should call the Embassy, he thought, and let them handle it. Or the police. But it was too late for that. He had walked into the trap. Chuk knew he had arrived. Like a fat spider, he was waiting and watching. If Durell left the sampan and tried to cross the garden to regain the alley, they would come for him. He looked at the canal. He might try swimming for it, but the two *kamoys* across the waterway could easily overtake him in their boat. He would be playing Chuk's game if he took either option.

He thought about it for another moment.

If there was no way out, then he had to go in.

The sampan was moored to a small wooden dock, secured by bamboo mooring poles thrust into the mud bed of the canal. Two stone steps led to a short path, no more than thirty feet long, between thick garden shrubs that opened toward the back of the house. Windows stared blankly and darkly toward him. There was a back door, a narrow veranda overhanging the water where the canal curved immediately beyond the mooring poles. He looked at the water. There was a slight drift of current down toward the veranda. He considered several alternatives – the back door, the porch, the wide sweep of the Thai roof eaves. In the darkness, he could not see anyone on the veranda or the roof, but he was sure that Chuk's men were posted up there, too. He wished again that he could go quietly away and let the Embassy or the Bangkok Police handle it. He owed James D. James nothing. James might be dead by now, anyway.

He had one other alternative, the old tunnel that led into the *klong* jar pit, from which he had escaped the other night. It was too far away. The men across the canal would get to him before he could reach the escape hatch up near the watergate market. He dismissed the idea.

"Uncle?"

"You are thinking," said the old man.

"We will pay you for the damages to your house."

Hu nodded slowly. "You will build me a new one?"

"I promise."

"What can I do?" the old man asked. "It was Mr. Chuk who killed my wife. He killed my youngest nephew, Tinh. Such a man is worse than a stinking toad. I will agree to whatever you say."

"Good."

"But you should not be too long. They will surely come here to the sampan if you wait here much longer."

Like most other small peddler boats on the *klong*, Uncle Hu's sampan had a low-powered outboard motor at the stern. Durell moved aft, under the low, curved overhead of the cabin, and picked up the gasoline can that rested on the bottom planking. There was at least a gallon still in the can – more than enough. In the cabin, he found a clay jar with a mouth small enough to be stuffed with a wick, which he fashioned quickly from a piece of rag among Uncle Hu's poor treasures. The old man watched him in silence, and poured another cup of tea for himself. Durell filled the small clay jar with gasoline, quickly braided a length of wick, and stuffed it down into the jar, plugging it tightly. He had matches in his pocket. To fashion the Molotov cocktail had taken only four minutes. Uncle Hu finished his tea.

"I agree. It is best if the house goes," the old man said quietly. "I am insured, in any case, with the Wu Fat Assurance Company of Sampeng."

"One of Chuk's outfits?"

"No."

"That's good. Then you might be paid. If not, I'll arrange for it in Washington. You stay here, Uncle."

The old man nodded. "And Mr. James?"

"If he is still alive, I'll get him out. If not, it makes no difference."

Durell stepped off the sampan onto the tiny dock, and went up the two stone steps in the dark garden. He thought he saw a movement in one of the windows. It took only a moment to light the match and touch it to the soaked wick. The flare of the match was like a bright little bomb in the night, but nothing to the effect of the thrown clay jar filled with Uncle Hu's gasoline. Durell aimed the bomb up at the veranda, watched the wick spark and burn as it flew through the air, and then he ran quickly to the right, around the tiny spirit house in the garden, toward the front of the building. The Molotov cocktail burst on the veranda and exploded with a mighty gush of flame. Instantly he heard a yell of alarm from someone inside the house. Footsteps thudded, halted, pounded toward the back. The night glared with yellow and red fire against the dry teak framework of Hu's house. Durell reached the front door, running fast, and crashed through. It was not locked. He found himself in darkness filled with the sound of excited breathing, curses, mutterings. He took his gun and fired blindly into the dark room, twice, and heard a shriek of pain and the stumbling thud of a body going down. He had been lucky. From the back of the house came the crackle and roar of the growing fire. Most of Chuk's men had rushed there from the vantage points where he had been waiting for his entry. Durell headed for the kitchen door, outlined against the glare of fire.

"Not so," said someone. "Very clever. But not clever enough. If you move, you die. If you wish to live a little longer, you will stand precisely still."

The trouble with Mr. Chuk, Durell thought later, was that he liked to practice his English too much. Nor was he as expert as he liked to think. He did not hold his heavy Colt .45 properly. He stood in the kitchen doorway, his vast frame silhouetted against the growing blaze on the veranda. Feet slid on the roof, scrabbling for a grip. There was none, and there came a sharp yell and the thud of a body falling outside. Durell smiled. He did not move at all, obeying Chuk's unwavering gun. He could get the gun, he thought, if Chuk remained poised like that.

"Come," said Chuk in his almost flawless accent. "We will leave. My car is at the end of the lane. I owe you a great deal, Mr. Durell, none of it good. You have dismayed me, I admit, by dismantling and destroying the results of a year's hard effort."

"Your caravan?" Durell asked softly.

"General Savag's."

"No, it was yours. Savag worked for you. And Miss Ku worked for you." He paused, as if struck by a thought. "I have a souvenir from Miss Ku, by the way. It has your chop on it."

The vast bulk of the Chinese quivered slightly. "We will go."

"Allow me to reach to my knee," Durell said. "It will be important to you, this memento I saved." Smoke billowed into the room behind the fat man, and two of his *kamoys* dashed inside and halted, then grinned and drew back as Chuk waved them aside. "I promise you, no tricks," Durell said.

"You have seen Ku?" Chuk asked.

"Oh, yes. Rather, she came to visit me, with the idea of framing James D. James. I didn't buy it, and she became annoyed enough with me to try to persuade me otherwise." Durell reached up his left leg and slid out of his knee-band the thin-bladed dagger he had taken from Ku Tu Thiet. He held it, palm up, hilt forward, for Mr. Chuk to see in the brightening light of the fire. "She tried to kill me with this."

Chuk licked his lips. His great moon face shook. "She would never give that to you willingly. It has been the property of my ancestors for many generations."

"Is Ku your daughter?"

"Yes."

"I thought so. And you planted her with Jimmy, to help you organize your drug-smuggling caravans. You used Savag as your front man and only pretended to be a subordinate yourself. But you, Chuk, were always the head of the dragon. It's not in you to take orders from anyone, or to settle for a small slice of the pie when you can gobble it all."

"What did you do with Ku?" Chuk whispered.

"I killed her," Durell said.

They were speaking in English, and the two *kamoys* who watched, their eyes glistening red with reflections from the fire, did not understand what was said. Above the crackling of the flames, Durell heard the distant wail of a siren, coming nearer. He looked down the muzzle of Mr. Chuk's heavy gun, which was dwarfed by the man's huge paw, and knew that at last the man's mind had snapped. He tossed the delicately carved dagger, hilt forward, toward the Chinese.

Instinctively, because the knife was precious to him, the fat man tried to catch it before it fell and was damaged on the floor. The tentative move was enough for Durell. He drove forward, caught at the man's .45, twisted it downward. The gun went off, its crash sounding enormous above the crackling flames. The bullet smashed harmlessly into the teak floor. Trying to knock aside Chuk's arm was like trying to break an oaken limb. He moved it just enough, and then drove his left into the man's big belly, feeling hard muscle under all the heavy layers of fat.

284

Chuk grunted and took a small pace backward. The flames outlined his huge form. Durell got his own gun in hand and started to bring it up, and Chuk raised one massive forearm and smashed at it, knocking it aside. The little knife fell to the floor. Durell heard the two *kamoys* shouting and he thought he heard another shot, and then he desperately drove his stiffened fingers into the fat man's throat before Chuk's men could interfere.

His efforts went home. Chuk's eyes bulged. He gagged and half twisted away, moving back into the kitchen, grunting and choking. Durell saw the two *kamoys* leap for him and fired once, and then again. There was an astonishing halo of flames around Mr. Chuk's big figure. He had caught fire from the flames that now enveloped Uncle Hu's kitchen. Still choking, he fell to his knees, outlined in a bright red aura. His hair scorched and burst into flames, along with his clothes. Durell saw the two thugs on the floor. His shots had put them out of the picture. There were others, he knew; he heard them shouting outside. Then he saw Uncle Hu's slight, aged figure come through the fire in the kitchen, moving fast, a large knife in his hand. The blade flashed, red, reflecting the fire, and then came up carmine with Chuk's blood.

285

"Come on," Durell gasped.

He pulled the old man out of the fire quickly. Uncle Hu did not seem to be harmed.

"That was for my nephew Tinh, and my wife Aparsa..."

Durell ran for the other room. The fire threatened to envelop the dry teak lumber of the house like an exploding bomb. He coughed, his eyes smarting from the smoke, and he crouched low to find cooler and clearer air near the smoking floor. There was a small woven mat on the plank floor of the next room, and he kicked it aside, revealing the trapdoor into the *klong* jar pit. He found an iron ring inset in the hard planking and tugged at it, heaving against the weight of the trapdoor.

"Jimmy?"

He saw dim movement in the familiar blackness of the confined space below. Jimmy James' haggard face appeared, a hand groping upward. Durell caught it, hauled on it.

"Hurry."

In a moment he had Jimmy James out of the pit.

29

They sat on the bank of the *klong,* some
hundred yards from the burning house, and
watched the Bangkok Metropolitan Fire
Department pour streams of water on the
blazing roof. A huge crowd had gathered,
safely granting them anonymity. Nobody
paid any attention to them. James sat with
his feet in the water, among the reeds and
mud, and drew in great, shuddering lungsful
of air through his open mouth. He was no
longer the elegant, debonair gentleman. His
pale hair was awry, his face was haggard, his
beige suit was in ruins. He looked as if he had
aged ten years.

"You were being used," Durell said. He
wasn't sure that the man could grasp what
he was telling him. "Miss Ku Tu Thiet was
Chuk's daughter. Chuk was the master-
mind of the whole drug-smuggling caravan
venture up in the Gold Triangle. Ku was also
General Uva Savag's mistress . . ."

"No . . ." James protested. "She –"

"She used you. She used Savag, too, just
as she manipulated you, knowing all the

security efforts that were being made and so was able to tell Savag, in order to outwit the authorities. But Savag is now dead. And so is Ku."

James' eyes were haunted. "You did it?"

"I did it," Durell said bluntly.

"Oh, you bastard. She was – she was so –"

"She was making a monkey out of you, Jimmy."

"My house – did you see my house?"

"They tore it apart, and planted a booby trap. Chuk's *kamoys* did it. They were looking for my report, maybe. Or intelligence data that they could sell to Peking's agents here in Bangkok. Anything for a buck, that was Chuk's motto. He wasn't one to leave a possible dollar lying around loose."

"My house – all my things?"

"How is it you lived so well?" Durell asked.

"I – I have an old uncle in Newport with lots of money. He sent me – he helped me out."

"We can check it," Durell said. "Just to tie up the last ribbon on the package."

James put his head down between his knees and retched. His long, thin body was convulsed with spasms of agony. Durell sat quietly beside him, watching Uncle Hu's house burn to the ground some distance away across the *klong*. He wondered what would happen when the firemen found Chuk's body and that of the two men he had shot. It was not his concern now. Rogers, at the Embassy, could take care of all that. He was aware of a great depression, a physical exhaustion that weighed him down like an overwhelming burden.

"What – what happens to me?" Jimmy James whispered.

"I don't know."

"I guess I've been a fool."

"Yes."

"Will I have to go home?"

"I should think so," Durell said. He stood up. His body ached all over. "It's finished here, Jimmy. We all make mistakes. Yours were just bigger than most. Maybe K Section will find a spot for you in D.C. I don't know about that. It depends on General McFee and how he feels about you."

"Have you filed it all in your report?"

"Yes."

"Did you have to?"

"Yes."

"You have no mercy, have you?"

Durell started to walk away. "It can be a

rotten business, sometimes. But you can't make mistakes and survive in it. Not for long, anyway."

30

It was dark and quiet in the room. An air conditioner purred, making hardly any sound. Durell had never been to the Slocum place before. There was a main house, and a small cottage down by the canal, and it felt like an island sanctuary against all the muted rumbles of Bangkok that surrounded them. Benjie had met him at the gate, wearing dark pajamas, and she had led him to the cottage. Mike, she said, was sound asleep in an upper bedroom of the main house, a good distance away across the carefully manicured lawns and shrubbery. Durell watched a pattern of pale light on the ceiling, sifting through the slats of the wooden blinds on the windows. The bed was big and wide and deep and soft. He wanted to sink into it forever. He had showered again, and was wearing nothing under the sheets. The coolness of the air conditioner was refreshing, and he should have been able to fall asleep instantly. But he could not.

"I'm glad you came here, Sam," Benjie murmured. She lay beside him, her body warm and silken. "Even if it's just for this last night. I don't think I can bear the thought of your leaving tomorrow morning. I won't go to the airport with you."

"All right."

"Do you think Jimmy James will be treated with some – some pity?"

"I don't know. McFee may use him at desk work. James is good at that. He couldn't do much harm in Washington."

"I feel sorry for him."

Durell said nothing.

"Sam?"

"Yes?"

"Are you sleepy?"

"No."

"Make love to me, Sam. Now. Please. I wish – I wish you could stay here, even for just a little while. I know it couldn't be permanent. I know I'm too wrapped up in the Thai Star businesses. Sooner or later, I'll probably go back to being what I was before you came into my life. But maybe I'll never be the same again."

Her body was impatient, growing imperative. He felt her weight over him.

The telephone beside the bed began to ring.

"Oh, damn . . ." she said.

"Don't answer it," Durell suggested.

"I have to – it might be business –"

"Forget it, Benjie."

But she picked up the telephone, lying across him to reach it. She listened, and he felt her soft, warm weight across his thighs, and then she wriggled about and laughed in the cool darkness and said, "It's for you, Sam."

"Nobody knows I'm here."

"The Embassy knows," she said.

It was Rogers. "Glad I caught you," the diplomat said. "There are several things you should be advised about, sir. Your hotel is taken care of. The dead Thai girl has been removed. Your name is off the register. There's no record of your being there now, and the Thai people have promised to be discreet."

"Very good."

"We've also kept you out of the affair with Mr. Chuk. However, an old man came to the Embassy and he asked us for money to build a new house. Says you promised it to him, sir."

"I did," said Durell. He felt Benjie's soft breasts press against his chest. She's changed, he thought, amused. He said, "The old man is Uncle Hu. He was a great help. It will have to be taken care of in Washington, out of the Y funds. I'll see to it myself, when I get there tomorrow."

"But you are not leaving Bangkok tomorrow, Mr. Durell," said Rogers. "I'm sorry, sir, but your plane ticket and reservation have been turned over to James D. James." Young Rogers' punctilious manner changed a bit. "There's a man who has gone through hell, I must say. Terrible thing. He's being shipped back to D.C."

Durell thought about his own past three days. He said, "What about my travel requisitions?"

"Canceled," Rogers said. "You are ordered to set up a new Bangkok Central, it seems. New files, new codes, radio, everything. New safe house, office, cover identities and occupations, the works."

"But that will take several weeks," Durell objected.

"I'm sorry, sir."

"I won't do it."

"Those are your orders, sir."

"To stay here in Bangkok?"

"For the time being, yes, sir."

Durell heard a soft giggle in his ear. Benjie's hands explored his body. He felt wide awake, suddenly. Benjie said, "Don't fight it, darling. Relax. Enjoy it."

He held the telephone in one hand, the other on Benjie's silk-smooth back. It was very comfortable in the room. The bed was big and soft. He weighed the phone in his hand for another moment, considering more objections to the impersonal orders from the young Embassy man.

Benjie reached across him and took the telephone from his hand and cradled it. Enough light came through the slats of the wooden jalousies to gleam in a liquid, pearly line along the curves of her hips.

"That's that," she said with satisfaction. "I've had my wish. You're not going away tomorrow, are you, Sam?"

"It doesn't look like it."

"How long can you stay?"

"As long as the job takes."

"Oh, that's good. That's very good." She sighed, and he rolled over and took her in his arms. She said, "Oh, my. You're not sleepy at all, are you? Oh, that's wonderful, Sam. Just right. You're going to help me, you know."

"How?"

"I'm going to make up lots of lost time," Benjie said.

Then she was silent.

The publishers hope that this book has given you enjoyable reading. Large Print Books are specially designed to be as easy to see and hold as possible. If you wish a complete list of our books, please ask at your local library or write directly to: John Curley & Associates, Inc. P.O. Box 37, South Yarmouth, Massachusetts, 02664.